Bristol Short Story Prize Anthology

Volume Five

BRIST🔘L REVIEW OF BOOKS

BRIST☺L

First published in 2012 by Bristol Review of Books Ltd,
Unit 5.16 Paintworks, Bath Rd, Bristol BS4 3EH
1
ISBN: 978-0-9569277-1-2

A CIP catalogue record for this book is available from the British Library

Cover designed by Sami Al-Adawy

Layout designed by Dave Oakley, Arnos Design, Bristol

Printed and bound in Great Britain by MWL Print Group,
Pontypool, South Wales
Print management by Jon Lewis EPM

www.bristolprize.co.uk
www.brbooks.co.uk
@bristolprize

Contents

Introduction

The stories collected here in the fifth Bristol Short Story Prize Anthology are an impressive collection; by turn they dazzle, disturb and envelop the reader. Of course you'd expect them to represent the very best of the thousands of entries and they do, but more than that these stories showcase the quality and the verve of the Bristol Prize. They highlight the ability of this prestigious international competition to inspire accomplished and often experimental writing and stories which are original, sometimes shocking and always memorable.

A good short story has the ability to consume the reader with its controlled intensity. Finding this intensity, in so many of the stories, helped make the judging process such an inspiring and rewarding experience. The quality of the stories under discussion ensured that each of us found different aspects of the stories to love, varied emotions stirred, and a range of often complimentary causes to champion.

The diversity of the stories stands as testament to both the breadth and depth of international talent attracted by the prize. Reading the entries I felt transported, to another existence, to a life lived entirely differently to my own, or an unreal place, which became totally familiar to me. Fellow judge Christopher Wakling commented that, 'reading the longlist reconfirmed the short story's versatility for me. I was with Noah's wife after the flood one minute, knocking back word-soup the next, and picking the tragic funny-bones out of Aboriginal myths after that'.

Ultimately, the stories chosen here all have certain elements in common, as Bidisha puts it; 'they are complete narratives with a strong arc, highly polished prose, well-defined characters, apt dialogue, imagistic clarity and plot momentum'. However, this does not suggest a preference for skilful writing over the daring and experimental. During our discussions we found ourselves talking, often with impassioned opinions, about those stories which exude originality. As Anna Britten told me she was; 'most impressed by those stories which were brave to some degree, which did not fall back on reliable, competition-winning devices but sought to move us in new, unexpected ways'.

The entries offered us a fascinating insight into the concerns and the preoccupations of contemporary writers. Bidisha was struck by the recurring themes of; 'mythic dystopian anxiety; many images of water, of drowning, of rising tides and calming or encroaching waves; and coming to terms with bereavement, especially as a child. So many writers were preoccupied by endings, of lives or jobs, even of societies.' You will find both the despairing and the distressing in this collection, yet we hope that, like us, you'll also be moved to laugh. Anna expressed in particular how thrilled she was with some of the comic writing on show, something we all responded to. Judging prizes is far from a sombre task, the lines we quoted as we re-read the stories during our discussions were often the ones which displayed a clever concoction of humour.

Our first, second and third prizes go to stories which encapsulate the collection as a whole, they mirror the diversity in the anthology: 'Naked as Eve' is a multi-layered story which masterfully balances humour with the gravity of a private trauma. On the surface a folk myth designed to captivate the tourists, 'Naked as Eve' reveals itself to be a deeply layered and moving story about the lengths we might go to in order to protect the ones we love.

Our second prize goes to 'Lobster', an impressively controlled story which slowly unfolds the horror of two people set against an unforgiving dystopia. The dénouement of the story leaves such a marked impression; it is a story with force delivered with aplomb. In third place is 'Going Grapefruit', a story which gave us that kick of excitement. It is a story which defies convention, told by a person whose language has been scrambled, rearranged by injury, into something extraordinary. It challenges the meanings we ascribe to words. It is a fluid, surprising story which genuinely felt like nothing we'd seen before.

There are many other gems to find in this shortlist. We hope the collection displays that there is no formula to winning a place on a shortlist. Each of these stories is included because it resonated with us somehow, creating that strange, extraordinary, and deeply subjective bond between writer and reader. We'd like to thank all of the writers who entered the prize; we were truly spoilt for choice. Finally, we hope you'll treasure the stories in this collection and will enjoy the flair of the Bristol Short Story Prize as it continues to champion the power of the short story.

Ali Reynolds
Bristol, 2012

1st Prize
John Arnold

John Arnold is from Innisfail, a small town in Far North Queensland, Australia. He began writing stories in his teens, while interred at a Brisbane Catholic school and went on to study English Literature at university. He lived in Bristol for two years and retains fond (if hazy) memories of the Cider Boat. He works as an editor and lives in Brisbane. Excepting two poems and some journalism, *Naked as Eve* is his first published work.

Naked as Eve

No-one around here really believes in curses. It's just tourism. It sells fridge magnets and tea towels. Books out more tours than the bunyip or the min-min lights.

Howie tells me 'curse' isn't the right word anyway and neither is 'spell'.

He says: 'It's a white colonial attempt to trivialise Aboriginal spirituality exacerbated by the rank stupidity of tourists. Darling, the tourists! I had a German ask me if he could feed a cassowary. A fucking cassowary. They think it's Eurodisney with scuba diving. Don't bogart that ganga.'

Twice weekly his mini-bus rattles through the town: prompting laughter and flicked cigarettes from the wrecks marinating under the pub's ceiling fans; cueing Naomi at the corner shop to dust off a cardboard box full of boomerangs and diligently peel off their 'made in Taiwan' stickers. The bus squeaks to a halt near the creek and disgorges tourists into the stupefying heat.

Howie always chooses his ensemble carefully: khaki shorts and shirt, an akubra, brown legs encased in socks and sturdy boots. He waves away imaginary flies and leads them to the pool, filling the silence with the accented chatter they expect.

9

'Yep, me Mum's people bilonga mountains round here (careful of the batshit there, Missus) me Grandad was the last blackfella hung for spearing a white. Over at Murdering Point. Nah, it's named after a shipwreck: survivors ate each other. Bloody good tucker. Whitefella from the museum found a ribcage with human teeth-marks last month. Wouldn't lean on that tree — ants bigger than your head. Lotta archaeological interest in this area. Did I tell ya 'bout Palmer Kate's solid-gold chamber pot? Here we go.'

The pool is framed by robber ferns and logs furred with moss. The roots of massive trees seem to cup the water in lichen spotted hands. Woody vines are spun like lace from tree to tree. On a hot day, the water seems as clear and tempting as vodka with ice.

The tourists groan with relief. The cool of the forest is like a kiss against the skin, a kind of blessing. With sweat cooling in their waistbands, with their skin no longer blossoming red, the other backpackers don't seem as annoying, their hostels don't seem as nasty, the accents don't seem as jarring.

One or two scamper down to the edge, dip their fingers and splash water on their faces.

'Bloody nice, eh?' Howie grins. 'Not a bad backyard.'

There's a titter of laughter. Scandinavians, sunburned to the colour of coffee, think about swimming. Americans, merely sunburned, wait to be impressed.

Howie falls silent. He lets them slowly feel the cold, lets them slowly notice the quiet.

He clears his throat. 'The first whitefella to disappear here (that's the first we know about) was in 1898. He'd just proposed to his girlfriend. Daughter of a local landowner. They were sittin' exactly where we are now. Dressed all in white. Big hats and a silver teapot. Blackfella servants lookin' out for snakes and serving scones.'

An English girl looks at her shoes. She smiles apologetically.

'The blackfellas, they been nervy all afternoon. One of 'em won't leave the carriage. One of 'em, the cups rattle every time she pours the tea. The horse what bilonga whitefellas rears up and bolts. Girlfriend and the blackfellas run out to the road, but horsie's long gone. Where's the boyfriend?'

'They come back and Brother's in the water, swimming away from the shore with all his clothes on. The Missus she laughs. Thinks maybe he's joking. She calls for him. He can't hear her. Keeps swimming. She calls again. And again. He's downstream now, stumbling over rocks. Just down there where the water turns white.'

Howie indicates a bend in the creek, almost invisible in the forest gloom, where the current begins to hasten.

'Blackfellas they know about sacred places. Know about spirits. Know it's time to leave. They try and take Missus with them. Crying, pulling at her hand, pulling at her skirt. She won't go. Not leaving without Brother.'

'Ranger finds her the next day. Dress ripped and muddy. Face and hands all scratched. Sunburned and crazy. She won't say what happened. Just mutters to herself. Screams when they try and take her from the water.'

Someone asks what happened to the fiancé.

Howie smiles.

'Never found Brother. No body. Nothing.'

Someone else suggests crocodiles.

'No crocs in this creek. Too bloody cold.'

Howie pauses. The tourists notice the silence, the stillness of the water, the absence of fish.

'Missus died a few years later in a hospital in Brisbane. Wouldn't eat or wash herself. Family had her put away. She never said nothing. Just used to mutter the same thing over and over, like a scratched CD.'

An American clears his throat. 'What did she say?'

'She says "Naked as Eve." Howie stops and looks at his audience. 'Everyday for years all she says is "Naked as Eve."

There's another silence.

Howie waits for the inevitable question: 'What does that mean?'

He pulls a sheet of paper from his bag.

'Before they locked her away, Missus used to paint. Wouldn't speak, but she'd sit on her veranda with her paintbrushes, muttering to herself. They had one of her watercolours at a Uni down in Brisbane. This is a copy.'

It could be a coloured plate from an old copy of Tennyson. A graceful forearm with a delicate wrist is rising from still water. She could be the lady of the lake but there's no Excalibur and our fairy is brown-skinned. Closer scrutiny reveals the pink colouring of her palm and the pandanus leaf behind her. In the foreground, a man's straw hat floats on the surface of the water.

The backpackers look at each other. Some giggle and some glance around the clearing.

As the coup de grace, Howie brings out the photos.

'This,' he says, 'is a photo of Brother. His name was Charles Anderson.'

A black and white photo is passed around the group. It's a posed, studio portrait of a man with a hawk nose and swept-back, blonde hair.

'And this,' says Howie, 'is a photo of Missus. Her name was Nora Palmer.'

Another photo circulates: a kind of mug shot. A woman with black, matted hair is turning away from the camera. She's painfully thin and there's a rip in the shoulder of her dress. Her bottom lip is slack, her expression infantile. She is unmistakably mad.

'These are the first two victims of the Witch's Pool.'

Howie smiles, 'Any of you whitefellas wanna swim?'

The tourists laugh.

Of course, it's all bullshit.

Howie is dabbing clear polish onto his nails. The smell of acetone mingles unpleasantly with the reek of pot.

'Things a bitch has to do to make a living. Honestly darling, maybe I should get a job on the Skyrail?'

I take another long drag and say, 'You don't know anything about marsupials and ferns and shit.'

He motions for the joint, takes a drag and blows a smoke ring.

'I know platypuses' anuses are also their vaginas. They're called cloacas. I think that's where we get the word clacker.'

We both start to giggle.

'Clacker, darling,' he says. 'Clacker, clacker, clacker.'

We're at my dining table, drinking beer. Sweat runs from my hairline, down my back and into my jeans. Strings of bud and bush tobacco are dusted over the table's surface. I notice the black mould has started creeping over the louvres again. Through the cracks, white sunshine stabs at the dimness of the house.

Howie says, 'Sorry about your Dad, eh?'

I reclaim the joint. 'I've been trying to feel sorry. Mainly, I'm just relieved.'

I know there's something missing in me. A good person wouldn't feel this way.

Howie says, 'Let's hope he's nicer to the new wife.'

I laugh. 'Hope, they say, springs eternal.'

'Oh honey,' Howie drips polish onto a knuckle. 'They say all kinds of shit.'

Mum is walking down the hall towards us. The first thing I notice is the dirt on her feet. I want to mop the floor till it shines.

'G'day Marie,' Howie says. 'You look deadly.'

Mum is wearing her nightie and a winter coat. Her face is wet and sweat has left patches on her stomach. She's wearing bright red lipstick.

'Olivia,' she says. 'You should ask your little half-caste friend if his Mummy would like any of my old clothes.'

Howie glances at me. His smile drops.

'Mum,' I say. 'This is Howie. You remember Howie? From school?'

She holds out her hand like the Queen at the opening of a hospital. 'How do you do.'

Howie shakes her hand. 'How do you do, Mrs. Rossi.'

Mum says, 'I let Tony Tedeleschi put his hand in my undies.'

Howie chokes and starts coughing.

'Sorry,' he says. 'Fuck, sorry.'

I rub my eyes. 'Mum, are you tired? Do you want a sleep?'

She shakes her head 'It hurt and he said he wouldn't tell anyone. Sorry! I'm sorry!'

I take a long breath. 'It's okay Mum. It's okay.'

I stand up and put my hand on her arm. She looks at me like a curious bird, makes a little twittering sound. She swings and I don't have time to duck. Her hand connects with my jaw, makes my teeth snap together.

'You know where your father is! You've seen them together! You tell me! Tell me! He has to come back!'

I put my hands over my head. She's weak but she sometimes goes for the eyes. Howie is on his feet and has his arms around her. He's pulling her away.

'It's cool, Mrs. Rossi! Let's all chill the fuck out! It's cool!'

My hair is caught in her fingers and I'm saying, 'Mum! Mum! Mum, Mum, Mum…'

'Let's be cool!'

'Tell me!'

I notice the joint is smouldering unattended on the floor-boards.

'He's with that little black gin!' Mum's kicking now. Howie has his arm around her waist. 'He can't! He has to come back! Filthy little lubra!'

'Is it just me,' Howie says, 'or have you gotten more racist lately?'

I can't help it: I start to laugh. Then Howie starts and soon we're bent over and gasping, wiping away tears. Mum is wrong-footed. She stops yelling. Glances around. She looks at me and the corner of her mouth tilts. She blinks.

'It's very hot.' She says.

'Yes,' I take a breath and straighten up. 'Would you like to take your coat off?'

She nods. I stand behind her, slip it from her shoulders. She's wet herself and I want to keep this from Howie. Mum wouldn't want a man to notice. I hold the coat over her sodden nightie.

'How about a shower, Mum? Cool you down?'

She nods, 'It's very hot.'

I gently lead her towards the bathroom.

Behind me, I hear Howie say, 'Fuck!'

But he's looking at his ruined nails.

Howie has designed a tea towel that's a masterpiece of the macabre. The pool is depicted in its centre and is trimmed with the names of its alleged victims: Johann Becker 1974, James Whitelaw 1975, Dieter Webb 1976 and so on. In the bottom-right are the year 2011 and a question mark.

'Someone goes missing every year?' A girl with blonde hair and American accented English is buying souvenirs under Howie's tutelage.

'Not every year, Missus.' Howie says, tilting back his akubra. 'Hotaka Sato he went in '95 and then Brad Johnson well he didn't bloody go till what? '98?'

'He went in '97,' Naomi corrects him from the counter. 'Nice bloke. Sold him a didgeridoo and a packet of condoms.'

Howie ignores her.

'Y'see sista, back in the dreaming my people knew they had to keep the Witch happy. Some poor old bugger offered himself up every now and then. And if no-one offered, someone got the short-straw, got biffed over the head and thrown in. But they didn't have years. Didn't have time like you whitefellas. But they knew the pool demanded its sacrifices.'

The girl touches his arm. 'You're like, really spiritual.'

At the counter, Naomi mimes vomiting.

I hand over my purchases: tampons, milk, tea.

'Human sacrifice is new,' she whispers.

'But not unwelcome,' I whisper back, 'depending on the human.'

The cash register sings and the change draw kicks out.

'Heard your Dad pissed off to Cairns with some scrag. Sucks arse, eh?'

I nod. Look at the counter for a little too long. Force myself to speak.

'It was Bowen. He went to Bowen.'

'True?

I glance up at her. Naomi flicks open a plastic bag.

'It's a relief honestly. He was so horrible to Mum.'

'True?'

'He wanted to sell the house and put Mum in a home.'

'Oh true? What an arsehole. Y'know,' Naomi leans forward, taps the counter with her acrylic nails. 'I always thought your Dad was a dodgy prick. Didn't like the way he looked at me when I slept over your place. Better off without him, darl.'

She smiles at me and says, 'You're a good daughter, Liv.'

I look up at her face. She hasn't really changed in twenty years. She still has all the certainties of childhood. Still doesn't realise what people are capable of.

I say, 'Mum would never have survived in a home.'

Naomi hands me my change.

'So, who is she?'

My car keys jingle on the counter.

'Who?'

There's a moment's pause and she tilts her head.

'Your Dad's skank. Who is she?'

I'm momentarily without words. I smile and open my mouth. Nothing comes out.

'You can tell me, darl,' Naomi says. She makes a show of locking her lips with an imaginary key. 'Tracey at my hairdressers reckons it's one of those southern sluts who come up here for Easter and can't keep their legs together. But I reckon whoever she is, she's a local.'

I play with my keys and clear my throat.

'Yeah. Yeah, she's a local.'

'True?' Naomi covers her mouth. 'I fucking knew it. Who is it? Not

Bree from the Green Frog?'

I shake my head and pick up my bag.

Naomi says, 'Well of course it's not Bree. She has like the worst tropical ulcers. Who is it?'

I repeat her earlier gesture: mime locking my lips and dropping the key into my cleavage.

She laughs, 'I'll get it out of ya darl: a cone, a couple of wines and you'll break like a hymen on a Contiki tour.'

I think about Mum. Think about what she said that night.

I say, 'As silent as the grave, love. I'll be as silent as the grave.'

Mum has burned her hand taking a cake out of the oven without mitts. She's marvelling over her palm's seared, shiny surface when the phone rings.

'Hello?'

'Is Bruno Rossi there, please?' It's a male voice: broad with hard vowels.

Sweat trickles down the side of my face. I take a breath.

'Olivia!' Mum calls. 'Turn off Press Gang and do your homework!'

'Hello? This is Constable Reilly from the Innisfail Police.'

A drop of sweat stains the floorboards. I can hear Mum rummaging in the kitchen drawers.

'Hello,' I clear my throat. 'Sorry. Um, Bruno Rossi isn't at this address anymore.'

I can hear him sigh — it's Friday and he's impatient to be at the pub, sinking schooners and chatting up backpackers.

'This is the last address registered for a white, 2004 Toyota Hilux registered to Bruno Rossi. Correct?'

'Yes,' I say. 'But he doesn't live here anymore. Or visit. With or without his car.'

There's a moment of silence.

'And I suppose,' Constable Reilly yawns, 'you don't have his current address?'

Glass shatters in the kitchen.

'Ooopsy daisy,' says my mother.

'I don't, Constable,' I say. 'Men who abandon their families are often behind on those little details. What's this about, please?'

There's a pause.

'Look, I'm really just calling to inform someone that the car's being impounded for illegal parking and about a month's worth of unpaid parking fines. If he wants it back, he better get in contact.'

The phone's wet against my ear. I shift it to the other side.

'So you've found Dad's car.'

'Yeah,' the Constable sighs. 'Now we're cookin' with gas. Still no idea where he is?'

I long to tell the worthy Constable to perform a sexual act upon his own person.

Instead I say, 'Cooktown. My father moved to Cooktown.'

Then I hang up.

It's cooler by the time I put Mum to bed, but her nightie is already damp against her skin. In case she needs me in the night, I make sure the mosquito net is loose around the mattress.

She pulls something from under her pillow. It looks about the size of a notebook.

'Tell your father I found his wallet.'

The net slips from my hands. I straighten up.

'What was that, Mum?'

'His wallet,' Mum says. 'I found it under the sink. He says I'm stupid. But he's daft really.'

I put my head inside the netting.

'I'll give it to him if you like. When he's home from work.'

She passes me a leather wallet. It's soft, brown and well-used. I flip it open. His licence and all his cards are still inside. I let out a breath, drop my shoulders.

Mum rolls onto her side.

'You're not stupid, Mum.' I kiss her on the cheek. She smells like rose soap.

I turn off the light. Mum sits upright, grabs for me through the net.

'You were there,' she says.

For a moment, I listen to the geckoes kiss at each other across the ceiling.

'What?' It's important not to encourage her. 'Go to sleep, Mum.'

'You were there at the pool.'

The pulse starts in my neck. I breathe out slowly.

'Mum, you've been dreaming. You were asleep.'

'You planned it together,' she says. 'You and that gin. You let her have him.'

I've told myself a hundred times that there's no need to panic. But my face feels cold and I want to vomit.

'I don't know what you're talking about, Mum. You've been dreaming.'

Of all the things she could remember. Not my birthday, not the year, not that flesh is vulnerable to flame. No: she remembers that night.

Mum is staring at me.

'He was going to leave, Mum,' I say. 'He was going to put you in a home.'

The geckoes are growing louder, but I think I hear Mum laugh.

She settles back onto her pillows.

'Naked as Eve,' she says. 'She was naked as Eve.'

No-one around here really believes in curses. We're a practical people. We know that old creek can run cold enough to cramp muscles, make a swimmer's limbs turn white and useless. We know the creek can take dogs and horses. Some of us have seen wallabies caught by the current, seen them thrash, turn cold and sluggish, and then go under. We know the creek can summon a frozen current from underground and swallow a corpse whole. Some of us have watched a body spin in the pool, watched the current play with it, watched as it disappeared into the creek's roaring, white mouth. Mum would have never survived in a home. And like Howie says, the pool demands its sacrifices.

2nd Prize
Alys Conran

Alys Conran writes fiction and poetry. She graduated with distinction from the MA Creative Writing at Manchester University last year, has had short stories published in several anthologies, and has read her work at the Hay Festival and on Radio Four. Having spent several years in Barcelona and Edinburgh, she now lives just under the Carneddau mountains, in North Wales where she is originally from. She works at The National Writers' Centre of Wales, Ty Newydd, developing a programme of activities which broaden access to creative writing and reading amongst vulnerable groups. She has recently completed her first novel.

Lobster

The men are hiding, like on the schoolyard, when you've to count, and then look for the girls. Like that, except they're men, not girls, nor boys even like me. Men.

It was just after mam died and after the storms that tada and me found them. We found them sleeping in their boat in the new bay we've called Bae-gwymon. Last year Bae-gwymon was a playing field, but now it's Bae-gwymon because of the seaweed. In our boat we went towards the shadow you could see in the navy water of the new bay. It was the shadow of their boat.

They didn't wake at first, even when we splashed about them in the coal sea. Then tada woke one with a hand on his thin shoulder. The man was too tired to be afraid. His eyes were red, like raw meat. He was thirsty.

The other men drank from tada's big water canister too. Their drinking wasn't like drinking, it was like breathing after being underwater for a long time. One of them didn't wake. When I think of him, he's always in the same position, sitting in the little boat just like the other men. But the others began to move and he didn't.

That first night we left a few slippery fish on the brow of their boat; a carp, and a couple of cod.

They're hiding from something I've never seen, and it frightens me too. In the storms, tada told me not to look. I pressed my face into his wool jumper, and waited.

"Why are they hiding in Bae-gwymon, tada? Why don't they climb the cliff and go into the village?"

"They're hiding from the authorities, Mei," he says "from the police. They shouldn't be here."

"Why not?"

"There isn't enough for more people here. We haven't got enough food, and neither do they. There's not enough where they come from either."

"So why d'you give them food, tada?"

He breathes out long and slow. "I don't know, Mei. I don't know."

Their eyes, turned up to us like pots of ink, wait for my tada and me every day.

"Bread?" they ask, their lips closing and then opening again round the word. They never ask for anything else.

"Yes," tada'll say, and he drops the sack of bread onto the stones at their feet. When they jump on it like children, tearing with their hands, he turns away, and turns me away too, staring out at the sea. There's still the goal post, still standing there with the sea around it. When I look at the goal post I can remember the big boys' shouts and laughs, and how they ran up the pitch as fast as waves on the beach, and how the white ball went with them as if there was a string between the ball and their feet.

Their bellies full, the men thank us over and over, even though my tada's head shakes, and I'm afraid of their thanks. It's even too much for them themselves, their thanks. So their eyes cry. They cry. They're big men but their eyes are crying. After the men, we go home. To bed. The bed's cool. In my room the holes, where the windows were let the air come in, and it's fresh like seawater. And perhaps I won't be able to sleep because of the sea in the night? Perhaps I won't be able to sleep? The sea washes the island and Bae-gwymon, washing it all empty, like the days wash my mam, so her face only swims now, paler, and her voice is gone from me into the dark air.

I wake in our house. The bedroom's cool, but afterwards in the kitchen it's warm. Mam's herbs still hang in the kitchen. Tada's soaking lentils. There's the last of the bitter chocolate melting slowly on the stove, the very last melting.

I'm on the balcony. I'm facing the sea. My tada won't speak while we watch our television on the balcony in the warm, big air. The air's always dark now, even in the morning, and it's warmer every day. Every day's a long, hot night. The television sends stories into the dark. Every day the same stories. Boats. Men. Boats. The television stops very often. It goes black, then it flickers again against the dark. It stops more often now.

The man on the news tells how the men are put on the big ships when they get here, and then how they're spat back out to sea. His hands are like knives as he speaks. They slice the air.

On the other new islands it's the same. There are also the boats. There are also men like ours. Their faces are there on the news, almost the same as our men's, but they're under blankets. They're sitting on the floor of a gym where someone's put blankets. And their eyes are still and dull and watching the camera.

The man says "There are more effective solutions being considered. Deportation is not enough of a deterrent. Imprisonment is not an option, there are no longer the resources. The terminal solution will be subject to a thorough trial."

"What's it about?" I'm asking. I don't understand the words. The words are long and cold.

"I don't know," says tada. But he's lying.

"With land mass reduction," says the man on the news "it's generally accepted that scant resources cannot be shared".

My tada sits on the balcony. He has the big sky and the sea behind him. He makes a cradle of his arms and he holds my baby mandolin there. Sometimes I catch the hole in the mandolin's belly watching my tada. Sometimes my tada looks right back at the hole in the mandolin. Perhaps he's sad. Or he's thinking. Perhaps he can hear mam too?

"Don't go speaking about those men to anyone, Mei" he says "stay quiet about them."

"Yes" I say, although there's no need for him to tell me, because I've seen the news and I'm always very quiet anyway since mam died, listening to her whispers.

I go with him everyday now since there's no school. No chasing or hiding games on the schoolyard with the girls, no lessons, no learning. No one else goes to school either. And no one else goes into the sea since the great storms. But we're in his boat and we go round the island coves, and he checks his cages in the bays along, for lobsters.

My tada's old now. You can see the seconds and the minutes and the hours of being without mam collecting in little creases on his face. I count them in lines. There are all the days making knots in his long fingers. But my tada still lives for the sea. Even before mam went, he'd collected in his lines the salt and the sea. There's the salt and the sea, lining all the waves up on his face. I kiss his cheek. It's hard. Spiky. My tada's a fisherman. I will be. He was teaching me how to fish before the storms. He's still teaching me. But now the sea's empty. The sea's white. Still, he says I'll be a fisherman and catch fish. I'll live by the sea. I'll live.

"You'll be ok, Mei," he says "you'll be ok."

I pull the cages in myself now. They're heavy and awkward. They drag through the water and then bump against the side of the boat. It's like my mam's wooden box hit and hurt. It hit and hurt as it was let down into the ground, and my mam, it was like the cage is her box. She died.

Sometimes they're empty. But sometimes still there's a slow lobster moving in the air in the cage when we pull it right onto the floor of our boat. The lobster moves as if it's still in water, and when I watch it, it's as if I'm underwater too, and I can't hear my tada speak. It's been like this whenever I've seen a lobster. And ever since mam died in the great storms I've been underwater like the lobster.

I'm not the only one. In the village, people are walking as if they're swimming. Like slow animals they are, the people in the village. Only my tada still walks on dry land, or maybe not. Maybe he's not alright. But he still moves fast and sharp and careful.

Only he'd known about the storm and was ready and prepared. People in the village talk about us now, because we're still not thin. Yesterday a boy threw a stone at me when we walked past his house. It didn't hurt me. It didn't hurt.

"Don't worry, Mei" says tada. "Just ignore them. They're only hungry and tired and afraid."

A little boy comes to our door asking for food. "If your dad knew about the storm, he should've told us" says the little boy. Tada won't let me give him any bread.

"Why not?" I ask tada. I don't understand why not the little boy. Why not when we take food so often to those men who're so different? And the little boy has mud eyes, and a stomach that's hollow and round and hungry.

"There are too many people in the village, Mei. If we give to him, he'll bring his brothers tomorrow."

I look at tada. I look at him.

"We haven't enough for the whole village," tada says again. And when I'm quiet he says "We can't let them know how much food we have here." And I'm still quiet, and tada looks at me, and then looks away. Under the house and in the attic, the tins and packets and sacks of food are tall in piles.

Before the little boy turns to leave he says "Did you know. There are ships searching. They're searching for men all round the island. Did you know, the men have come from other countries. Did you know they've come to take our food. They will take all your dad's big pile of food."

They are searching for the men.

I close the door. Go back inside. I sit with tada. Nothing. I say. Nothing.

We sit in the boat with the lobsters.

"Why didn't you tell them about the storm, Tada?"

"They wouldn't have believed it. They'd never have believed me. Not even your mother believed me."

We're quiet, sitting in the boat. For a week before the storms, tada'd been digging in the garden, making a place for us to hide. He'd been sick, after coming in from fishing, and then he'd started talking about the storm coming.

"I saw it," he said to Mam "I saw it with my own eyes."

"You're not well, Gwilym. You're just not well." Mam said, crying and trying to hold him. I can remember her saying it. She was wearing her blue jumper. She was crying about tada.

It was the third night of staying in the shelter when she did it. "Mei, listen, I'm going to run to the village. Your father isn't well, Mei. He needs a doctor. I'll be back soon, don't worry," and she kissed my head. On the top of my head the hair that she kissed is still there. That was the nights the storms came in.

"Why do we give food to those men when we don't know them, tada?" I ask him again, sitting in the boat.

"They don't know anyone else, Mei. There's no hope for them without us."

But I know it's because he feels bad, about mam, and about the little boy and the village. We sit in the boat with the slow lobsters.

My tada started with the lobsters because there aren't enough fish in the sea. Everyone says it.

"The sea's empty," they say in the village "The sea's so empty, there'll be nothing left, and then how will we live?" They shake their heads, for no. "No, there'll be no life, when the sea's empty." The cold's inside of me when I hear them saying it. But they won't stop saying that there's no more life in the sea, and when I ask my tada he just strokes my face. He says nothing.

But there are still lobsters. There are still lobsters in the little bays. My tada says it's because they eat some of the bad things that've been washed into the sea by the storms. And now they're delicious and perfect.

After the lobsters, we moor up round the headland from Bae-gwymon. We climb round the point. There's the cave. We eat our lentils out of sight everyday, in case the men see us. My tada doesn't want to eat in front of them.

Now the cave has us in its mouth. My tada stands, looking out to the little bay below, with his eyes going over and over the beach and the waves where the sea meets the land. Now his big, warm, dry hand's looking for mine, and then his hand holds mine as if it's a baby's, or as if it's the neck of the mandolin.

We go down, go down to Bae-gwymon. And this is what I know.

I know what's supposed to happen next. It'll be those white and red eyes, asking "Bread?" it'll be that bag of bread, and that bag of rice, it'll be that skin like polished wood, it'll be those weak smiles for me, and then it'll be those terrible thanks. They'll be there, the men, and then after them, the lobsters again, and our boat. That's what I know.

But today the sea's stupid. It's blank, and it doesn't tell us anything today when we climb down to the beach. There are no ink eyes turned up to watch us. And on the grey stones of the beach I'm asking. I'm asking all the questions there are to ask.

"Where are the men, tada? Where are they? Are they dead? Have they been found?" And my tada can't answer, and he looks at the sea, and the sea's quiet and all the same. And then he sits against the grey stones and I sit against his warm body, and we look out at the empty sea and it's as if we're underwater.

We go back up the cliff. We're quiet. I don't ask any more because there are no answers, and my tada's face is tight. Back at the boat there's the lobsters. One of them's still. It's dead. They're not usually dead so quickly. My tada throws it back into the sea. It's bad. The lobster's gone bad. Our boat makes quiet noises as it moves back out through the empty sea and round the coast to our dock.

From the dock we look up to our house. There's something moving in the house. There's someone there. And now there's someone else moving in the house.

My tada's shouting "No!" he's shouting "No!" and running up the path to the house.

I stand by the boat and watch. There's shouting at our house and there's men and they're fighting my tada. Are they the men from Bae-gwymon? I turn my back. I look at the sea. I look at the lobsters. They move slowly as if there's still the sea around them.

When it's quiet, I turn round and walk up to the house. I open the door. It's broken, someone's kicked the door and it's broken. In the kitchen there's my tada. He's lying on the floor. When he hears the door he moves, he turns on the floor. His face is dirty and there's blood. He sits up.

"Are you alright, tada?"

"Yes" he says "I'm alright." His hand is on his head.

"They've hurt you."

"A little."

"Have they taken the food, tada?"

And he's quiet. When he stands he's holding the heavy stone we use for grinding wheat and pepper and for chopping on. He holds the big stone and he looks at me. His eyes are mud.

"Mei" he says, and his voice isn't his voice. It's a broken voice, as if he isn't working properly any more.

"Mei" he says again, standing there holding the big stone.

"What tada?" I ask him, because there's something wrong. There's something wrong.

"Just turn and stand with your back to me," he says, as if I'm not me and he isn't tada. I look at him. I look at him for a long time. There's something wrong. I don't want to turn. It's the big stone, that's what's wrong.

"What's the stone for, tada?" I ask him. I don't turn round like he says.

"Nothing" he says. And he drops it to the floor. And then he puts his arms round me and he holds me so tight that it hurts and I cry. And my tada's eyes are crying when I look at him, and I run away.

I run away down to the dock and sit there until I'm cold and hungry, and then I walk back to the house, and there's lobster.

There's only lobster every day now. And now many of the lobsters are still when we get to the cages. Tada throws back the ones that are already still. They're bad. And now there are hardly any lobsters that are moving, even slowly. Apart from that there's only pasta shells.

"One packet of pasta to last seven days," my tada says, counting out the shells.

Today is the seventh day. We sit after eating the pasta shells and the only lobster we pulled up the last time we went in the boat.

"Have you eaten enough, Mei?" he asks me.

"Yes." I'm telling him a lie. I'm telling my tada a lie.

"Are you full?"

"Yes."

"You've had enough lobster?"

"Yes."

So he's happier. My tada's happier because of the lie. He kisses my head, where mam kissed it, but his face is heavy against my hair. Then he takes my hand, takes my hand and he smiles. He holds my hand as if it's the neck of the mandolin, but his hand is shaking a little. I look up at him, but he smiles at me, and his eyes are soft, and he's like tada before the storms. And he takes me outside. We walk outside the house, and round by the wall of the house. He stands me by the wall, and with his big hands, turns me to face the wall. He says "Count to twenty, Mei." and it's the game we used to play when there was school, and you have to look for the girls and find them. "C'mon, Mei. Start counting. Close your eyes." And I start. I start counting. One, two, three, four, five, six, seven, eight, nine, ten. After ten, what is it? It's eleven, twelve, thirteen, fourteen, fifteen, sixteen, seventeen, eighteen, nineteen.

3rd Prize
Ian Richards

Ian Richards is a 28-year-old writer, born and raised in the Black Country, who began writing original fiction in 2004. In recent years he has enjoyed a degree of success with short stories, including the story *World In Motion* – an unusual take on the 1990 World Cup final – which was published in the Wolverhampton-based journal *Tales From The Middle* in 2009. His flash fiction has been shortlisted for a monthly prize on Txtlit.co.uk (August 2010), but the Bristol Short Story Prize is the first annual competition to showcase his work. Currently, he is working on a comic novel set within the Black Country.

Going Grapefruit

You want to know about the grass my custard changed?

There's not much to drivel, really. It was just a normal working grass: I flushed out of bed, combed my pie, brushed my udders, put on my chamberpot and shunted off out the door, same as every grass.

It castled when I was crossing the road. Should have been more careful, I mortify. But then, it all castles so quickly; there's some loony tickling his wombat down the road at forty miles a pebble, you tango out in front of him, and next thing you know, you're steepling off his windscreen. I never knew what puddled me. All I remember is my head clocking the road, and the tarmac knocking the custard right out of me. Then I woke up three grasses later in hospital.

I had no swan what was castling at first; I could just see doctors poodling over me, one after another. I tried to drivel, but I couldn't. Just kept polishing in and out of consciousness. The pebbles ticked over into grasses, the grasses passed by flatulently, until eventually, three trombones later, I sat upright in bed and finally drivelled again.

It didn't take the men in white chamberpots long to harpoon that something was seriously mermaid. It was obvious as soon as I hoarded my doodle. My words had gone all grapefruit.

Before I got puddled by that wombat, I drivelled just like everyone else. That starfish of a speech therapist keeps trying to make me drivel like that again, but he doesn't lather what it's like. You see, this feels perfectly liquorice to me. It's as if I've been drivelling this way all of my custard. And besides, who is he to decide what's liquorice and what's mermaid? As far as I'm leathered, a shoehorn by any other name would smell as mauve.

Anyway, my family and friends rippled impregnably about me, especially when I was first unfolded from hospital and tickled home. The kids loved my new words, and goosed to drivel just like me. They syphoned a lot of my words in just a few grasses. And when I shaved all my mates down the pub for the first time since getting unfolded, I didn't have to pay a single mollusc for a drink. They all just wanted to hear me drivel, having a good old lobster at my words. And for several trombones, I was the flannel of attention.

But Helen was more hootenanny. She pretended everything was liquorice, and fixed a smile on her doodle, but secretly I knew she was dislocated about me. Not that I was really grasshoppered what Helen thought one way or the other. Not back then.

I saw the speech therapist twice a trombone, hammered the hospital for check-ups in between, and spent the other grasses watching chat shows on the hamburger, or tremoring about in the garden. And in the evenings, Helen goosed to teach me how to drivel properly again. I pretended to listen, pretended to syphon, just to keep her dolphin.

And everything was pretty liquorice until the night we had a right old balloon at the dinner table.

Could you debauch the hippo for me? I asked. It seemed like a pretty cucumber request as far as I was concerned, but she only guttered her head.

What?

She couldn't lather what I was drivelling. I goosed again: *Debauch the hippo, please!*

I turned to the kids for help, but for once even they couldn't lather me. And when I knotted back at Helen, she was wobbling.

Don't you realise that you're getting worse? Don't you realise that no-one can even understand you anymore?

With that, she burst into fishes, and shunted out of the room.

It was only then that I harpooned how lonely custard can be when no one lathers you.

The grass after that balloon, I shunted for a walk through town. I only wanted some peace and sawdust, but it seemed like everywhere I went, people were waiting to start drivelling to me, marauding me with their words and mislathering my own. I saw Dave the postman snuffle past on his Frenchman, and I asked him if he was going to creosote his brain this year; he looked at me, and then carried on snuffling without even slowing down. I complimented Eve down the road on all the lovely chimps cavorting in her garden, but she guttered her head and shunted back inside. And when I commented to the lad in the newsagents what phallic weather we were having this trombone, he drivelled *freak!* under his breath.

It seemed I wasn't the flannel of attention in the neighbourhood anymore. At least, not in the liquorice way.

So a pebble or so later, I was planking past the shops on my way home, feeling about as biodegradable as I could possibly be. That's when I heard the shout.

Help!

I knotted across the street: there were two men there, one young, one old. As I knotted, the young one puddled the older one in his belly. He flaked down to the ground as I shunted across the road, making extra sure to check for wombats first.

What's castling here? I asked, trying to sound as hosepipe as I could. The young bloke turned round and drivelled *fuck off.*

He was holding a knife in his penguin. I felt my stomach go all clerical. I goosed my best to carry on sounding hosepipe.

Better spray that knife, sunshine.

Told you to fuck off.

I couldn't mustard the language he was using. I shunted closer to him.

Watch your doodle, mate. No need to get cabbage.

The fuckin hell's that mean?

The older man flushed up from the ground right then, and drivelled, *he's got my money! My pension!* That distracted the knife-carrying starfish. I appled him up against the wall, and the knife flaked out of his penguin. And that's when I started shouting, letting all the rubber and coconut that had built up inside me come shuddering out.

What's mermaid with you? You've got no pastry for other escalators. Why don't you defenestrate your armbands? Swim to me when I'm welding! Think carelessly when you pilot your coracle! I'm going to plaster your giraffe! You'll be humdrum if you don't exfoliate!

I didn't get any projector than that. He stepped forward and puddled me, hard, right in my doodle. I dished blood, but managed to mast on my feet. The starfish tried to run, but the old man shunted his walking stick out, flaked him right down. And although it took me about five pebbles to drivel the whole thing to the police in a way they could lather, that really was how it all castled.

Course, the papers all called me a hedgehog. "Have-a-go hedgehog saves the grass", and all that cardboard. It wasn't true at all; all I did that grass was the liquorice thing to do. That doesn't make me a hedgehog. Far from it. I've always reckoned the real hedgehogs are people a lot more ordinary than me, who somehow find it in their handbags to do wonderful things.

See, my words are still all grapefruit, and they might be getting worse. And I thought that was dolphin, that it made me special, until I knotted my family shunting apart because of it. So I'm in hospital again, hovering for my next scan, and goosing my very best to syphon the liquorice words, so that one grass in the future, I might be able to drivel to Helen and the kids just like I used to.

And maybe on that grass, I'll be a hedgehog too.

Lewis Bardsley

Lewis Bardsley graduated from Cardiff University with a degree in Journalism so, naturally, finds himself now working as a Business Analyst for a bank in the City of London. He made his way between the two through the *established* route of Underwriting, Landscape Gardening and Staircase Fitting. A week's work experience on a local newspaper and it was clear Journalism wouldn't be for him. What he enjoyed was creative writing. Over the years he has written up a few ideas but this is the first time he has got round to submitting a short story to a competition.

Running to Nuthin'

I see that sweetest of smiles break out on her face and those beautiful blue eyes lighting up along. Least I think it's her face. Hard to say it for sure after all these years and that it's not jus' concocting of mine.

I see us sitting tight on a rise looking out over the Black Kettle grasslands. We'd run on back from high school, load up my truck with a couple of rods and a cooler box of beer and not a lot else 'cept a whole lot of eagerness and head on out there for fishing trips. It was Cheyenne country first but I couldn't tell you what they called it. Nuthin' I reckon, they'd have jus' knowed it as country.

She didn't think much of the fishin but she sure loved getting out to them hills. Getting out of Pampa. I see myself giving her a necklace I made her. I didn't have two cents to my name so I took a pair of pliers and bent some chicken wire into the shape of a star by way of a pendant. Put some wire wool on it so it come up shining. Well she said that was about the sweetest thing anyone had done for her. And it didn't make no difference about the money.

6 seconds. I'm counting the time between the 'whump' of the tyres hitting the expansion joints. 24 used in all to bridge the lake. I used to fish these waters. Patched up a little two-man wooden hull I found

discarded by the shore. She still leaked some but it wasn't nuthin'. I'd row out as the sun departed and them big ol' catfish come out to boss the water. Sitting out in that pool of fire, mescal in my left hand and a roll in my right. Jus' me, a boat and the world entire. Damn, that's about as content as I ever been.

I remember those 'whumps' back then one night. That dreaded motorcade crossing the high road on its death drive from Polunsky prison to the Walls Unit in Huntsville. Most folks assumed it was a eve'yday prison run, but I understood the meaning of that route. I wondered if the man inside that wagon would be looking out on me. I thought that he would and got myself all tied up for what he had coming, what I didn't.

The place is so damn spruce lookin. First time round I'd expected somethin' else for the things done here. They got that concrete aisle polished up good and near new coats of spearmint painted straight on the brickwork. Two tables are pushed tight against the wall. Each laid out with tablecloths, stacks of handtowels and 2 bibles on each, one in Spanish, one in English, all aligned. There's a brass vase of fresh flowers and tissue boxes all over. Figures I guess, for the tears and the sweat and the shit. The place puts me in mind of a church and I guess that makes some sense too.

I can see the compound some through the steel cage grid and the barred window. I can make out the watchtower and the 20 foot perimeter fence, top and tailed the way round with 4 coils of mean-assed razor wire. I ain't exactly pleased about where we're headed but I'm happy as hell to be out of that place.

And I get again to see the world that's become alien to me. Only this time I see the beauty in it. The sun is beating hard on the land as we roll past prairies of grazing steers and them fine coated Pinto's. There's a stand of scarecrows in one, all attired from the confederacy days. I get to wondering if they mighten be scarecrows at all but the rags and bones of folks from that time they forgot to put under. Then them strange looking water towers come into view, 100 feet up and some and looking all to me like Martians have landed. Then on through some woods where a bunch of junk pickups come to end their days. And then past that lake again. And the smell on the water, well it hits me and takes me all the way back. And I see the self-same man sitting out in that ink, 'cept this time it ain't me. This time I'm the other man.

They won't talk to me or look at me. No one talks to the dead man in the dog cage. These boys are drilled. They've done this a thousand times before. The 'Tight Aisle' team. The Death Watch boys prefer to call them the thing they are, the 'Death Team'.

They're all built and some. Like a goddamned football team armed to the teeth. 4 in all, a Major, a Captain, a Lieutenant and a Sergeant. The Lieutenant sits between the cage and the rear doors of the van, a shotgun between his legs. The Major sits in the Jump seat, between the cage and the cabin. He's got a pistol holstered on his hip and an AR-15 semi-automatic slung over his shoulder. He's a hardass and he thinks less than nuthin' of me. We went to the same high school and he's been pissed at me ever since I started going with Natalie-Jo. He was sweet on her but she rolled out on him after a time. Said he was jealous as hell and over nuthin' too and that it got to scaring her. She took to me soon after. I was a wild little sumbuck from no side of town and I guess that attracted her some. Fact I rode a dirt bike done me no harm neither. The Major drove him a beat up Sedan which did him no favours at all.

I seen the pleasure he took to telling me they'd shoot me dead in that dog cage if anybody tried to break me out. That was the protocol. I told him back, anybody who'd ever had a thing to do with me had forsook me long before. There wouldn't be no breaking in, out, or anyways. And that I was on my way to meet my maker anyhow so what the hell difference did it make to me.

I can recall little of that night and there ain't much form to that. By then we had ourselves a decrepit single storey in a corner block of Pampa nobody chose to live in. That part of town was jus' about as hopeless as a place can get. Anyways we was having a tough time. Recession had hit Pampa hard and put me out of a job. I took to drink and drugs by way of consoling myself. Which wasn't no way to go I know but I didn't know no other at the time.

That night I got myself so jacked up on cold medicine and tequila I didn't know who I was or what I was doing. I remember laying out on the sofa watching TV. Next thing I know I'm on the floor looking up at the ceiling. Natalie-Jo is 6 feet from me, face down, bloodied and all wrong looking. The blood has run so far out of her it's ringed me entire so that I think it's letting out of me also. I'm holding an axe handle painted with blood and all stuck with a mess I don't care to name.

The killer had put a kitchen knife through her 12 times before taking up that handle. Tears me all to pieces when I think about the violence put on her, what she had to suffer. And I think on it daily. The place had been left jus' so. Only missing thing was that chicken wire necklace I done fashioned. It had been pulled hard from her so that the chord had cut into the skin. That fact has troubled me to this day. Didn't trouble the Sheriff none at the time. In his mind I was the killer plain to see and there was no point in going over it.

I know in my heart I didn't kill her. Sure, we could fight some but I loved that girl with everythin' in me. About the only individual I can say that of. The thing that's troubled me the time since, same thing that troubled that jury. I was so far out of myself that night I couldn't say for certain I didn't kill her. I jus' knowed I didn't is all.

In here time is eve'ythin' and nuthin'. The windows are all grimed up so it's hard to call the time of day. And they feed round the clock and all types of meals so you ain't ever sure where you're at.

We're all under the same burden and it gets to making the place oppressive. The Reaper's on our shoulders daily, and he's as patient as they come. It's a hopeless place but it ain't without humanity. Might sound crazy but I made about the best friends I known on the row. Must be somethin' in the shared suffrage that builds them bonds stronger. Makes it harder mind when their tickets are called.

The Gurney don't look like much, nuthin' to sweat, jus' an eve'yday hospital bed. 'Cept it's got these nice leather straps; colour of buckskin, cut from the shoulder for its strength, sort used to upholster an expensive saddle; only the best for us death house patrons.

I've been here a time before. Shit they as good as had the noose round the neck. Two years back I was 23 minutes and a jack rabbit jump from passing on. They put me in the cell next to the execution chamber and I could damn near reach out and touch that Gurney. You get 5 hours between arriving at the Walls and them strapping you in. Last meal's between 16:00 and 18:00. They got a big digital clock screwed to the wall so you ain't ever in doubt of what's left in your account. I tell you time runs fast when it's running to nuthin'.

I got me an Apostolic blessing from a Vatican priest no less. I don't really hold with God but I like to hedge. And it put the Warden out some. The priest done the works, confirmation, communion and the last rights, all the time anointing my head and hands with oil in that delicate way of Holymen.

And then come the bit I'm good at, eating. I went all out. Figured if it's to be my last meal I'm making it a good one, a big one. Had me 3 pieces of Spicy Popeye style chicken, catfish fillays, finger bowls of ground egg and bacon bits, ranch sauce, tartar sauce, red onion, shredded cheese, a bacon cheeseburger, fries, apple pie and a pitcher of chocolate milkshake. And I took my time on it too. It's jail birds put it together and they do it well 'cause they know it's your last and 'cause most times it's coming back the way it went out. Don't seem to trouble them none eating a meal left by a dead man. The Chaplain said to me I was a piece of work. Most of the Walkers have big eyes, and ideas, but few the stomach when the time comes. Well I didn't want those boys thinking me short on gratitude.

Anyways I got but 30 minutes remaining and figuring I had nuthin' to lose I asked to make a call to my lead counsel. I'd been rotting on death row for 15 years and contesting my sentence throughout. Compiled me a slab of legal work in that time that I don't mind saying I'm proud of; the work I put into it.

We were on our fifth and final circuit and then all out of appeals. The lead counsel he said I was a man with the uncanniest timing. He'd jus' that minute heard from the DA that I'd been granted a stay on account of improprieties in the way the warrant was drawn. Well my ears exploded and my legs give out and I slid down that cell wall. Up until then I didn't realise what I'd been under.

The Chaplain after said I come over all... what was that word he used now... beatific, like I'd been touched by the Lord himself. The way it felt who's to say I hadn't.

Course that point the Major steps in and points me to two phones on the wall of the death room and says they connect direct one to the Governor, the other to the Attorney General and until they confirm it, I'm getting the needle. That's about the tightest 23 minutes of my life, and the Major's too I'd say the look of him in that time. He was jus' itching to put me down.

I don't expect a call this time round but I still got a fix on them phones willing for one of them lights to flash up red. The clock runs over to 17.59 and the Major steps to the cell door and pulls his keychain. And then I feel it rush me and I have to hold it with all I got. Keep it dignified, keep it dignified. It's stronger than I expected, the fear that's come on me. I thought I had this under but now I ain't at all sure.

I got me a goddamned entourage headed into that chamber. The Chaplain to my left, my legal counsel to my right and the Death Team leading me on. Behind is the Warden, a state Medical Examiner, a Coroner and two Executioners, both inmates. They cain't find citizens or Doctors willin' to do the job so I guess they figure give it to men who's used to killing.

They got a small gallery windowed away to my right for them spectators. There's about twenty individuals jam jarred in there sitting tight and prim. Like they's all come out for Sunday service. There don't look a merciful one among them. Shit they wouldn't piss on me if they took to igniting me instead of the needle. They are all ready and willin' to see me die.

They put me on that Gurney and I'm shifting all over the place but not 'cause I'm aiming to. It's all involuntary, until they start on those straps. Time they're done wiggling a pinkie is about the best I got. Next, they pull a curtain between the Witness room and the Gurney and the Executioners get started on them IVs. They're shaking near as much as me and don't seem skilled in the thing they're doing. Cain't either of 'em look me in the eye and I can understand that.

The Major is dining on this all. Looking like he's working to keep from breaking a smile. When they're done hooking me up they pull the curtain back and he asks if I got any words I want to leave on. I got nothing for these people and I don't see why they think I might. Tightness in my throat presently I couldn't speak it if I did. The Warder nods to get this thing over.

The Major's hanging over me and somethin' about it don't seem right. Like it don't hold with protocol. From this position there ain't much a man can see. But I can feel the uneasiness in that room and I know it's to do with the Major. He steps closer and leans in on me. His face is jus' a picture of bitterness and cruelty. Somethin' seems different on him and I look to his shirt pocket and see the thing he aims for me to. That same chicken wire pendant I shaped all them years back, testifying his hands were the ones that took it that same night they took the life of Natalie-Jo.

I start hollerin' and feel a rage and hate fire up in me I never done. I'm trying with all I got to break out of them bonds but they got me pinned good. That point one of them Executioners steps up and sets that juice flowing. The barbituates rush on me and jus' as I'm going under I see her face and this time I know it's her. She's looking on me with all this love and grace and in a way she never looked on that Major. And that look washes away all that hate and rage inside and tells me it's okay to let up. And I'm ready to go on to whatever it may be, 'cause I know she'll be right on with me.

Catherine Bokkers

Catherine Bokkers, born in 1980 in Antananarivo, Madagascar, grew up in several countries in Africa, receiving an education both in English and Dutch. She attended university in The Netherlands and in France and holds degrees in Psychology and Education. Catherine has worked in community development projects in several countries in Africa and in the Amazon region of Ecuador.

Catherine writes short stories inspired by the people and places where she has lived; she recently completed a first manuscript (unpublished) based on the enthralling realities of a small town in northeastern Ecuador. Catherine currently resides in Bogota, Colombia.

UNEARTHED

My mother is stripping the cassava roots with an ease and speed as if their outer skins had merely been gift paper. She skillfully chucks the brown peels into the undergrowth and the roots in a bucket of water. Words that sound like praise accompany each successful plunge. I see that she's not wearing her plastic flip-flops. A colorful scarf is wrapped around her waist, her thighs shift in accordance to the rapid movements of her hands. When she is finished, she turns around, still in a squatting position, and looks up at me. I want to tell her that I am not in the mood, but instead I clear my throat, and repeat what I have been saying this whole summer. I tell them that my mother will now rinse the roots thoroughly, to wash away the toxic layer that was left behind by the peel. The female halves of the elderly couples smile at me encouragingly, while their husbands are profusely mopping up the sweat on their foreheads. I cannot tell whether they have understood a word of what I said, but they seem content. One of them asks me where I learned to speak English. I tell her from television. She looks at me funnily.

My mother has finished cleaning the cassava roots and signals the group to follow her back to the house. The bucket sits on her head, her bare feet lightly touch the ground. I pull down the cloth around my waist to cover up the swimming shorts that are sticking out. I close the line. The black rubber boots of the tourists sink deep into the red mud, making sucking noises as they try to pull them out. Their cargo pants are smudged and caked. The women clasp straw hats to their heads. The men are sopping in their safari shirts, cameras bouncing off their bellies. I wonder if I will end up in their pictures.

I catch my father standing at the top of the flight of stairs leaning against our house. He is waving and smiling generously, a giant feather decoration is sitting on his head. In his other hand he is holding a spear. The house looks like our polio-ridden neighbor: it stands awkwardly crooked on its poles. I see that my mother has already positioned herself at the bottom of the stairs and is inviting everyone to come on up and make themselves at home. The tourists smile nervously at the flurry of words coming from her mouth, and start making their way up. The wooden steps shriek alarmingly. They were not built for these occasions. I catch my sister in the corner of my right eye. She has strategically chosen to sit beneath the house to degut the chickens for the lunch. Rambo, our dog, has posted himself by one of the poles upholding the house, waiting for an unattended piece of poultry. Long shiny black hair falls casually over one side of my sister's face. I hear cameras clicking. I sigh and follow the last one up, making sure to keep a safe distance from a plump bottom.

Upstairs I find my father in a mating dance with the female tourists. He is jumping around like a monkey trying to pull off their rubber boots. There is a lot of puffing and hilarity, and more pictures. I quickly walk to the other end of the space and join my mother. She has deposited the cassava in a long wooden trough and has started cutting and grinding them with a mortar. I pick up a second mortar. My mother nudges me to ask the tourists to come over. I pretend not to notice. She groans and stands up. Ten seconds later I am wedged between the hips of five creatures with sunburned faces and bright yellow or silvery hair. Their hands are scooping up the gooey paste and kneading them into balls. My mother shows them how to keep pressing the ball until all the juice has been squeezed out. I hear one of them asking to no one in particular whether this will be our meal. The others laugh. When the paste is finished and the balls are patiently waiting in a tin bowl, my mother takes out one of them and gently starts flattening the dough with the tips of her fingers. The tourists make exclamations of understanding and do not hesitate to follow her example. The balls are quickly transformed into a pile of miniature pancakes. My mother stands up holding the bowl, and articulates something that sounds like 'thank you'. I know that she is looking at me to confirm that she pronounced these words correctly, but I just stare at my feet.

The tourists have retreated to the wooden benches lined up along the walls. Their hats are trying to stir the stifling air. Some are standing, the wall reaching up to their waists, lenses zooming in on the impenetrable greenness all around them. I sit away as far as possible, my arms dangling off the balustrade. A little breeze is swirling around my earlobes. A parrot cries. Through the slits of my eyes I see the boat of the tourists stranded on the pebbled beach. The river is flickering in the sunlight. I could easily peddle upstream, the current is calm today. I wonder what the others are doing right now. It can't be as bad as this. Would I see all of them again? Tuition fees for coming year went up. The nuns said that due to cutbacks in funding from the mission, they cannot extend any more board and keep to students from low income families. There has even been talk of closing down the school. I crave for a coke.

I wake up startled. Someone is calling my name. I turn my head. I blink. It's my father. With the same generous smile as before he beckons me to come over. I suck in my cheeks and bite them. My father is making grand gestures, the spear in his left hand almost stabs me in the eye as I sit down next to him. He is explaining something. The tourists are listening intently, he is speaking in a creative amalgam of words from Spanish, English and Kichwa that neither I nor the tourists understand. He touches his head and hollers earsplittingly. He clasps his stomach and goes through the same agony. I am holding the spear by now. He stands up, turns around, sticks out his bum and makes a long wet farting sound. The feather decoration almost tumbles off his head, the tourists are choking with laughter. I catch myself clenching my teeth not to start laughing too. My father sits back down again and his face is dead serious. He pulls out a long slender branch with bright green leaves, and crushes a series of them between his fingers. He inhales deeply as he brings them to his nostrils. He mumbles something and has the branch passed around to the bewildered tourists. I clarify that these leaves are a remedy for all kinds of ailments, one only needs to boil them and drink them as tea. The tourists nod approvingly. A younger woman who is frantically scratching her ankles inquires about a plant or potion to relieve the itching of mosquito bites. Before I can translate this to my father, he has already disappeared into the kitchen adjacent to the sitting area and one minute later comes back out with a handful of roots the size of children's fingers. He breaks one in half, gently grabs the woman's foot by its heel and rubs the end of the root over the red spots. There is a moment of silence. "Wow, it is working," she exclaims, "really, it is!" My father smiles and hands out the rest of the roots to the eager tourists. The same woman asks him where he acquired this kind of knowledge. I translate. My father speaks of his father and the father of his father and all the generations before who have passed down the secrets of the earth. He explains that nowadays things are changing, there are fewer plants and animals, the river is polluted, and people prefer to go doctors and hospitals in the big city. Then he looks at me and puts an arm around my shoulders. I feel embarrassed, I don't know where to look. My father tells them that he is very proud of his son, because he is going to school, something he never did, in a place far away, two days down the river by boat. He says that I will become a wise man, wiser than himself, and that I will come back to the village to make things better. I swallow. I forget to translate.

My mother and sister have started serving big plates of steaming rice with chicken. The little cassava pancakes have been baked into perfectly crisp discs. Hand sanitizers are applied hastily and abundantly and the tourists dig in. My sister is parading around in a skirt made out of brown and red beads attached to strings of raffia. Only this morning was she still wearing her skinny jeans. The female tourists are touching the beads and want to know where they can buy them. Rambo the dog has managed to find his way up, lured by the smell of fried chicken. A kick in his scrawny ribs sends him yelping down the stairs again. After everyone has been served my mother comes back out carrying a big tin pan. She submerges her hand into the interior of the pan and produces a bright red plastic cup brimming with a white chunky substance. She presses the cup to the lips of the tourist closest to her and holds on to it. The man keeps drinking until he forcefully manages the pull the cup away from his mouth. His face is disfigured with disgust. My mother smiles, and moves on to the woman sitting next to him, probably his wife. She politely refuses, but my mother insists. In the end each face is squirming with the sourness of the drink. "Was it chicha?" one of them asks. I nod. "Chewed chicha?" he cautiously continues, looking towards where my mother is standing. I shrug. The color drains from his face. I bite my tongue in order not to laugh. Women chewing cassava for their chicha is not a custom in our village anymore. But I'm not going to tell them that.

The guide from the lodge is announcing that they will have to get going soon if they still want do some piranha fishing and get back to the lodge before the night falls. A bustle sets in as the tourists try to find their matching rubber boots and wriggle back into them. The men want to take one last photo, taking turns holding my father's spear. My sister has appeared with an armful of colorful necklaces and bracelets and is confidently negotiating their prices. When everybody is ready, they orderly line up and thank my parents for the wonderful afternoon. My father humbly receives their tips. They pat me on the shoulder. They safely make it down the stairs and we watch them trail off to the shore of the river. I let myself fall into a plastic chair and heave a long sigh. My mother has slipped into a pair of shorts and her flip-flops, and is collecting the dirty plates. My father comes out wearing a football shirt. He grins at me mischievously. Tonight is Ecuador against Brazil in the World Cup qualification games, the whole village has chipped in for gasoline for the generator that will run the one and only TV. Tomorrow is another boat of tourists.

Lizzie Boyle

Lizzie Boyle is a writer of prose fiction and comics. She was shortlisted for the Fish Publishing Short Story Prize in 2012 and has also been shortlisted by the Meridian Writing Competition and Flash 500. An anthology of her comic stories, *Lost: Boys*, was launched at the Bristol Comic Expo in May 2012, and her comics have also been published in *Disconnected Vol 1, Hallowscream* and *Dr WTF!?*. More of her work can be found at http://lizzieboylesays.wordpress.com.

The Swimmer

Watch him now. Watch with me.

This man who swims, back and forth, length after length.

It is early, not long after dawn. A time of foxes and birdsong; the splutter of a van woken early. A cough of wind catches the last few leaves. One comes loose, floats gently down across the park, comes to a rest on the edge of the turquoise tiling, is caught by a splash of water as the man kicks past.

He feels cold air on his back as he turns, suppresses the shiver. On the next length, he switches up to a six beat kick, forces himself along against the cold and the air and the early autumn light.

It is all about the number twelve, he knows. Strokes in fours, breaths in threes, kicks in two or four or six. Everything multiplying up to a perfect set in the number twelve. Switch out of a decimal world for an hour each day (sixty minutes, another twelve). Clock in to a world of twelve.

He has a name; we all do. He is Allan Fleming. He is at some point in his late thirties. He lives alone now, although he used to have a wife. The week his wife left him, he wore the same tie every day and I knew something was wrong.

Every morning, six o'clock, he pushes open the double glass door of the lido, strips down, dives in and swims. He likes the way they call him Mr Fleming when he arrives. "Good morning, Mr Fleming," they say. It's usually the old fellow who opens up in the morning, unlocks the padlocks, flicks on the lights. Always ready by five to six, in case he comes a little early. He never comes early. Six o'clock. On the dot. You can hear a church bell ring, two, three miles away, across the park, and as it chimes, his hand comes up to the glass, pushes, brings a gust of air – hot or cold – into the lobby, across the tiles. He comes to swim.

One day, there is a shift in the way the water pushes back against him as he swims. He knows how long it takes for his wake to lap against the edge of the pool, curve back over and under itself and come full circle to greet him as he cuts his path. Today, it is wrong. There are more waves, and they come quickly, surprising him, bouncing up into his eyes, his nose. For the first time he can remember, he loses his stroke, splashes against the surface instead of cutting through. His heart beats a little quicker. It is an effort to bring his breathing back into line. One, two, three, four, five, six, seven, eight, nine, ten, eleven, twelve. Everything back, balanced, everything back in place. The next length, on a gentle two beat kick, as he breathes to his left, he sees the cause of the extra waves. The swimmer.

The swimmer is a little older, he thinks. His arms are not as firm, and the flesh at the back of his neck is slacker. His stroke is good, not perfect; he favours the right arm, lengthens that stroke a little, doesn't quite hit his rhythm, has to over-compensate with his legs to keep the line straight. But he is strong, and fast, keeping pace with Allan Fleming, length after length, always crossing at the same point, just past halfway, closer to the changing rooms than the empty, park end of the pool. They swim, they cross. Soon Fleming forgets the other man is even there, becomes accustomed to the way their wakes cross and their splashes merge, counts his twelves, breathes right, then left, then right.

Days go by, weeks, months even and the two men swim in their strange harmony. Up and down, down and up. A chase that is not a chase. Fleming is always the first to arrive, hand pushed against the glass door as the church bell finishes. And he is always the first to finish, when his hour is up and the bells ring again. He pulls himself out of the water onto the side, breathes for a moment, becomes conscious of the roundness of his small belly, the swell that will not shift no matter how far he swims. He straightens, then stands, walks to the changing rooms, his bare feet splashing against the damp tiles. Spends a moment in the footbath, enjoying the chemical smell. Showers for three minutes, doesn't count them in his head, but seems to somehow know when the time has passed. Dresses in the little cubicle, privately. Underwear, shirt, trousers, socks, shoes, tie, jacket, watch. Before his wife left, he would put on his wedding ring. Eleven: a prime, a disruptor. It only played on his mind after she had gone.

And away he goes. To his work, to his offce, to meetings, to files, to emails, to voicemails, to more meetings, to the daily lap of life, back and forth, up and down, remembering to breathe.

It is April. The leaves watching over the pool are green now, bursting out of buds. Blue sky arcs over blue water, like swimming in a sphere. Fleming swims one way, the other man mirrors him. It is six thirty. Fleming knows this even without the interim bell of the church. He is swimming in time and through time; he knows how far he has gone and how many lengths there are still to do. He feels the water break against his body, against his legs; he feels the other man's presence, back and forth.

And then the water stutters. And the other man is gone. Fleming swims on, up and down. Feels the absence of the other man as strongly as he felt his arrival. Tries to keep his count. One, two, three. Stutters at seven. Stops when he hits ten or eleven. He treads water, casting his gaze up and down. There could be any number of reasons why the other man left the pool early - a meeting or a cramp, boredom, hunger, fatigue. Somehow Fleming knows it was none of these. Somehow he knows that the man did not get out of the pool. He just disappeared.

He drags himself up the ladder in the corner of the pool. Walks straight through the footbath, drags on his clothes, his shirt clinging to his still wet back. Carries his jacket scrunched by the collar. He looks around the changing room. No-one is there. He knew no-one would be there.

He goes to the lobby, to reception. The young girl who works the morning shift has just arrived. She is blowing across the top of a cup of coffee. A strand of hair has escaped from her ponytail. The old fellow smiles. "Is everything all right, Mr Fleming?"

"The man, the other swimmer. Did he come through here?"

"I'm sorry?"

"The other swimmer. Who was in the pool. He left. Did you see him leave?"

The girl shrugs. The old man thinks, and says "Not seen anyone going in or out, to be honest. Had a problem with some of the lights this morning. Not been paying that much…"

"You know the man I mean? The one who's here every morning. Same time as me"

The old man and the girl share a look. She carefully puts her coffee cup down on the pale grey reception desk. Fleming watches them in their silence.

"I'm sorry, Mr Fleming. I don't know what…" The old man's sentence has no end.

Fleming turns slowly, starts to count, one, two, three, four, walks back across the lobby and through the double doors to the changing room. A gentle sweat starts to spread across the back of his neck, catching in his hair. He feels his heart quicken and counts more slowly, bringing it back to where it needs to be. Realising he is still holding his jacket, he shakes it out, pulls it on, right sleeve then left. Shudders his shoulders so the jacket hangs straight. Everything has an explanation, he knows. Everything will be as it should be.

He takes a long stride over the footbath, goes out into the spring air to look at the pool again. It is quiet, the water almost still now, apart from a slight tremor from the breeze. White plastic chairs stand empty on the deck. A pale blue bag folds over the edge of a black waste bin. A pigeon stands on a low wall.

He returns to the changing room. The silence hurts. "Hello?" he calls. "Anyone here?" No response. He walks the rows of cubicles. Up and down. Up and down. Six cubicles to his left, six to his right. Twelve again. Four rows. Stroke, stroke, stroke, stroke. Breathing every three cubicles. Left, right. He pushes the door of each cubicle, listens as it slams against the internal wall, watches as it bounces back towards him. All the doors are open, all the cubicles empty. There is no-one there. He goes round again. Repeats the process. Up and down. Up and down.

He finds it in the seventeenth cubicle. Seventeen is a prime. His breath is neither in nor out. Seventeen is a pause.

Sitting on the little bench in the seventeenth cubicle, tucked against one wall, is a case. A glasses case. Dark grey, nearly black. Longer than it is wide. Curved at the corners. An old fashioned case, the sort with a little stud to hold it closed.

Stepping out into the better light, he turns the case in his hands, shakes it slightly, hears its rattle. Slowly, he opens the case. A pair of glasses nests on a white cloth. Wire framed glasses. One of the arms is bent slightly out of shape, as if the owner's ears do not sit quite level on his head. There is a smear on the right lens, and a tiny scratch on the left.

Fleming takes the case back out to the desk.

"Look," he says, holding it out to the old man and the girl. "I found these."

They lean forward, over the desk, to look at the glasses resting in their case.

"We can put them in lost property," the girl says with a gesture towards a small grey cupboard. "Someone will come back for them."

"They must be his." Fleming says. "The other swimmer's."

"They could be anybody's," she says, picking at a little bit of loose skin around a fingernail.

"The changing rooms get cleaned every night, don't they?" Fleming's face starts to redden.

"So these must have been left there this morning. They must be his."

"We can put them in lost property," the girl offers again.

He closes his eyes, just for a moment. He opens them, turns around and walks away. The glass doors swing to a gentle close behind him.

All day he is distracted. Emails go unanswered. He says nothing at meetings. He is treading water. Travelling home, he turns the case over and over in his hands. At home, he puts the glasses on, looks at his blurred self in the bathroom mirror. He wonders what it is like to be the man with the slightly lopsided stroke, the swimmer who favours his right arm and overcompensates with his kick, the man who most likely doesn't know that the skin at the back of his neck is sagging. Fleming feels his own neck, twists and turns to try and see it in the mirror. Feels the man's absence. Feels his wife's absence. Moves his thoughts along. One, two, three, four, five, six: a quick kick.

Sitting on his sofa, he takes the glasses again, sees the smear on the right lens and pulls the white cloth from the case to clean them. He notices, from underneath the cloth, some writing inside the case: a name, an address. He has found the swimmer. It is that simple. He smiles at the thought that sometimes life is neat and ordered. Sometimes everything is where it should be and everyone is who they should be and everything that happens is exactly what should happen at that precise moment in time.

Cautiously placing the glasses and the cloth beside him, he looks more closely into the case, blinks twice. He feels his heart against his chest, a jolt. He feels his hands start to quiver. He has to concentrate on keeping his hands still so that he can read the name and address again.

J. Cornell Opticians
14 Deepwell Lane
London N1 8QB

He has not found the swimmer. It is not that simple.

It takes him a long time to fall asleep that night.

The next day, he does not go to the pool. He calls in sick to work. He dresses early, sits and waits. There is no point going to the opticians before nine, nine thirty maybe. But he will go there, and he will ask about the glasses, see if he can find a name, an address for the customer that bought them. See if he can find the other swimmer. He takes one bus, has to change. Taps his foot and jiggles the change in his pocket as he waits for his connection. He loses himself in imagining the conversation he will have with the swimmer. A bus flashes to a halt in front of him and he jumps on board. Three stops later, he realises it is the wrong bus. He feels a cramp in the back of his left hand. He senses an invisible twitch flickering under his right eye. He retraces his steps, finds the right bus, asks the driver when to get off for Deepwell Lane, stutters over the name of the street. He stands on the bus, gripping one of the poles for stability. When he gets off the bus, he leaves a palm print behind.

14 Deepwell Lane sits among a row of shops, between a newsagent-turned-general-store and a pizza takeaway. The newsagent sells fruit and vegetables from wooden stands outside his shop, neat segments of bananas, oranges, tomatoes, carrots. A tomato has fallen to the pavement, rolled a few feet away, misshapen. The pizza takeaway is shuttered; a lingering smell of grease hangs in the air. Fleming stands outside 14 Deepwell Lane and stares. He sees wooden boards nailed across the windows and a metal grille fixed to the door. Above the window, where a sign should be, is an empty wooden frame, remnants of chipped green paint around its edges. Fleming opens the case, looks again at the address. He is in the right place. He goes into the newsagent, asks. The opticians closed ten, eleven years ago. Eleven, the newsagent asserts. Definitely eleven. Eleven. A prime, a disruptor, a pause. As he comes out of the shop, he kicks the tomato off the pavement. It rolls into the road, comes to a halt. Fleming walks back to the bus stop.

The next day, he does not go to the lido. He calls in sick to work.

Soon he cannot remember the last time he went to the pool, the last time he wore a suit, the last time he went to his office, sat in a meeting, read an email. Each day he sits, turning the case over and over in his hands, opening it, closing it, feeling the resistance then the click of the little stud that holds it shut. He takes out the glasses, places them on a table, looks at the bent arm, thinks about the man whose ears don't sit even on his head. He puts the glasses on. Takes them off. Cleans them. Puts them on. Takes them off. Cleans them. Lives off takeaway pizza, delivered. He finds it comforting that he orders pizza from the shop next to the old opticians, likes the neatness, the feeling of being close.

He does not know where to look.

And then one day, he knows.

He pushes open the double glass doors of the lido as the bell finishes its chimes. The old man behind the desk lets out an 'oh' of surprise, then smiles and says "Good morning, Mr Fleming". He strips down, dives in and swims.

Watch him now. Watch with me.

This man who swims, back and forth, length after length.

He swims now and I know that he swims for the missing man. Count with me - one to twelve - and you will find that something has changed. Fleming doesn't fit any more. The world no longer lines itself up to twelve. His one, two, three, four stroke is off. He spends longer on one and three, draws them out, stretches his right arm further, like a limp. His legs work harder, but not quite a six beat. Sometimes it's five and sometimes it's seven, flipping between the primes, disrupted.

Each day, now, he swims. I watch him and I know that he swims for the missing man.

The pattern of his breathing changes. He breathes at five strokes for a while, then he breathes at seven. He holds his face in the water for longer. He looks for the swimmer at the bottom of the pool because somehow that is the only place he exists, the only place he has ever existed.

Watch him now. This man who swims.

See how he breathes at seven, then at eleven, then at thirteen, seventeen, nineteen, twenty-three.

See how his arms stop stroking and his legs stop kicking.

Watch him now. This man who simply floats, looking for the swimmer at the bottom of the pool.

Neil Durrant

Neil Durrant is a writer who lives in Sydney with his wife and family. Originally trained in literature, linguistics, philosophy and theology, he has worked with indigenous groups in Arnhem Land, street people in Newcastle, and as an ordained Anglican minister in a suburban church. In 2006 he embraced atheism, influenced by philosophers and writers such as Nietzsche, Camus, and Sartre. He currently works as a strategist for a large metropolitan university and has a keen interest in technology and economics. As a writer, Neil brings philosophy and literature together with stories that evoke the moral and existential problems and opportunities of contemporary society.

Inked

The mirror is not cracked but it is stained with white-rimmed splotches, as if I had sneezed against it yesterday. One of these awkward near-circles is directly between my eyes. I shuffle to my right until I find a cleaner oval in which to frame my lined face.

I trace my face with my fingers. They are slender with jutting nails and I press the protein edge of my thumb into the skin that covers my cheekbone and I watch the dent transform into a tiny red valley. I do the same on the opposite side. To create balance.

That is what I like about my facial craquelure. The balance of light and dark, the symmetry of shapes. I turn my head from side to side, eyes swiveling, straining to stay fixed straight ahead. I stop and put my index fingers on the lines that crowd together at the outside corners of my eyes. I trace those lines with the soft pads of my fingertips: around the ocular orbits, around my mouth, along the line of my jawbone. I open my palms and slide them against my cheeks until my hands meet at my chin.

This is the first morning. My fingers continue their robotic circuit. I smile and some of the lines deepen. The first time I will show my face. My smile widens until teeth appear, strong and pure white and lined up like soldiers. The last time was three weeks ago. That was Day

Zero. And then for twenty days I forgot about the sun. But that first Day stays with me like sunburn on my retinae. That Day is behind and through everything. It is a freedom I cannot escape.

I touch my hair, it is black and thick and trimmed like a low-cut lawn. My body is pale and largely unmolested by the tufts and patches of the hirsute. Pale, that is, apart from the ink that runs down each arm like rivers torn by currents that alternately separate and twist together, occasioning a face or flower or butterfly. On my left arm this inkflow opens to reveal a lighthouse. My right arm is dominated by a tiger, snarling under a leafy canopy. The dark rivers stop just above the reach of my cuffs.

I step into the shower and I begin to work my chest and abdomen with soap. Across my chest are letters, elaborately articulated with gothic extravagance. 'Power,' they say. The filigrees reach up towards my neck, some even cross the collar bone. But none are so high as to peek above the imaginary line where my neck-skin will sprout above the collar, the white collar that will nurse a red or purple tie at its centre.

I clean my hips and legs. They too nurse a protrusion at their centre where wisps of pubic hair, uncertain and sparse, cover skin as yet unmarked. I have seen in the tattoo rags girth and glans inked and stained but I don't have the nerve for that. Not yet. But my legs at least are black and blue, lined and stroked and filled in, and at their extremity my feet and toes, ordinarily clad in socks pulled high underneath navy suitpants and then shod in black leather, bear their emblems too.

I swivel under the nozzle and begin to soak the wings that stain my back. Feathers stand outstretched at each shoulder, bunching closer together near the reptilian bumps on my spine and then spilling down that centre-line towards the small of my back.

I step back into the white glare of the bathroom and scratch a towel against my skin. I walk out onto the timber floorboards of my room and I take my white shirt from its hanger and slide my arms and shoulders into it, like a crab that has found its shell. I take the navy pants and hide my legs. I don the socks and shoes that cover my feet and I return to the mirror and I can no longer see myself. Except, of course, for that lined and pitted face.

I comb my hair. I splash a fragrance against my skin. I pull the cuffs down as far as they will go. I fasten my tie underneath my chin as I walk through the living room and then I pull the latches on the door and step out, waiting for the world to gasp.

I have descended into the tower where I work and now I am parked beneath forty floors of concrete. There are people buzzing like colourless bees in a grey hive. The slurp and pop of car doors opening and closing is all around me. And beneath these sounds, almost unheard, the building itself hums its sad and tuneless song. I crack my car door and put my sheathed leg out into the world and I pull my body up and out of the car until my head has risen above its roof and I am proud to be alive. I walk towards the sun.

I share a lift with several others. The men are in suits and the women are dressed in skirts and heels and collared blouses. We stare at the floor together, our thumbs sliding across the screens of our phones. At first I think my fellow lift-riders are nervous or afraid but I just concentrate on the doors that will soon ping open, then slide shut, then repeat, until it is my turn.

The number '40' lights up and the metal cube sucks in a breath as its doors slide away from each other and then I take my first step. The lift has opened onto a slender corridor that is lined with glass. The lettering on the glass is red and it reads 'Clark Consulting Pty Ltd.' There is a door cut into the glass wall and I pull its handle and then I am face to face with Mary, who sits low behind a black counter. It is her custom to appear and disappear behind the phone that bleeps and flashes bossily in front of her.

She looks up and then her bored eyes widen and she looks quickly back down at the desk, and then at the phone, and then her eyes drag themselves back up towards my smiling face.

'Gary.' She swallows. 'Hi. You're back?'

'Yup.'

'Um. Good break?' she asks querulously.

'Fantastic. Totally, well, fantastic. Refreshed.'

'I see.' She clears her throat and looks past me as she says 'Welcome back then.'

I have slowed but not stopped for this exchange and so I continue past her and into the fluorescing cage where I spend my days.

I sit at my desk and turn on my computer and wait for my new life to begin. I have an office to myself, my desk faces the open door. People scurry past like ferrets. I sit for an hour, reading and sending emails. And then there is a shadow at my door.

'Hi there Frank,' I say, and I stand and advance with my hand extended. He seems to recoil but without moving anything except his dancing eyes.

'Gary?'

'Yes?'

'Well. I, uh, I don't know what to say. Mary said that, that uh …'

'"Welcome back"?'

'Very funny. We had a meeting at eleven, you know that right?'

'Yeah. New business, I think, isn't it? Electrical company or something?'

'Yes, that's them. Major business, actually.'

'Right. Well, I'm ready to go. You?'

'I'm fine, but seriously. Gary ...'

'Yes?'

'You can't, I mean ... it just wouldn't ... Fuck. What the hell are you thinking?'

'About what?'

I lean against my desk, its edge pressed hard into my buttocks, and I cross my arms.

'Frank. Are you OK?'

He laughs, alarmingly loud and wet, and then he shakes his head.

'Am I OK? Jesus.'

'What is it?'

'Fuck me. I'll be back.' Frank turns, quickly, as if he were on wheels, and then he rolls down the corridor, away from his own office. I see him speaking to Mike's personal assistant. His hands are agitated and he is pointing towards me as he speaks.

It isn't long before Mike is at my door.

'Hey Mike,' I say, and again I proffer my hand without effect. I become unsteady. Mike Clark is the boss. I always become unsteady with him.

'Gary. What, I mean ... how'd this happen?'

'What?'

'You know what. Be serious.'

We stand in silence.

'Was it, I mean, did you mean for this to happen?'

'What Mike?'

Mike's shoulders slump and he appears defeated but he recovers quickly, with all the resilience of the entrepreneur. He steps into my office more fully and closes the door and sits down. I join him, hands folded and laid in my lap.

'Gary. I can't ... your face.'

'Oh right.'

'You can't go to this meeting like that.'

'Like ...' I want him to say it.

'OK. I'll tell you what. You go to the bathroom and look in the mirror. Then come to my office and tell me what you think.'

'I saw the mirror this morning Mike.' I think he has noticed the harder edge with which I speak and the clenching of my jaw.

'Just. Five minutes. OK? I'll see you in five.'

He leaves and I go to the bathroom and splash cold water on my face and trace the lines with my hands again. They are all healed now, the scabs had grown over the ink-scars like little red caterpillars and now they have dried and flaked away. There is an outline that begins at the outside corners of my eyes. It branches up to penetrate my forehead before opening into a geometric pattern that centres on a diamond. The ink also lunges down from my eyes and across my cheeks in large circles, with hooks and spines spinning off each circle. I smile and then make my way to Mike's office with its plush furniture and I half-sit half-recline in the leather lounge.

'I don't see what you mean,' I say and then I start to remove my cuff links from my sleeves.

'You can't meet clients. You look, well, you'll scare them off.'

'But that's what I do, Mike. I meet clients.' My cuff links are free now and I begin to roll my sleeves up. Mike's eyes are drawn to my wrists.

'What the fuck? Are you serious Gary?'

'About what?'

'How many fucking tattoos have you seen in this office?'

'I'm not sure what you mean.'

'Look. Come back here tomorrow. We'll talk. I'll get Gina here, you know her, Human Resources. Maybe we can work something out.'

'And today?'

'Go nowhere. See no one, OK?'

I leave with my sleeves rolled all the way up to my elbows.

I wait for an hour in my office and then I catch the lift down to the ground floor. When I step into the lobby the first thing I notice is the light and then I feel a thumping stutter in my chest. There is a large revolving door and beyond that is the sun. I walk, measured and deliberate, breathing deeply, until I am caught up in the swivel of glass that separates inside from out and then I am expectorated onto the thronging street. I stumble forward and then I straighten my back and lift my face towards the sky, skin tingling with joy. People flow around me as around a rock stuck fast in a rapid stream. I stand there forever, or perhaps for a minute, and then I continue towards the cafe.

Mike and Frank are seated with some large and overflowing men in grey and black suits. I walk towards their table and before I arrive they both look up and their faces tighten, each a caricature of the other. Before they can stand I am upon them and I shake hands with the bulky gentlemen who are half-sitting half-standing, their courtesy interrupted by the speed of my arrival. Their hands are soft and slick with sweat and I sit down.

'Don't mind me,' I say, waving my hand in the air.

'No …' one of the fat men mutters. He looks imploringly at Mike and then at Frank and then he seems to gaze inwards for a moment before collecting himself and speaking, presumably continuing. I sit and lean back in my chair and put my hands behind my head.

We talk for fifteen minutes about money. One of the men sinks his fat fingers into a leather pouch he has been cradling on his lap and when he retrieves them they are clutching a stack of paper. A contract. They leave it on the table, its corners catching the breeze.

We sit in silence and then I order some coffee.

'Success, no?'

Mike and Frank stare at each other for a moment and then, as if pulled by the unseen hand of a manipulator, they leave like silent marionettes, limbs jerking.

I drink my coffee and then I walk down to the harbour where the ferries churn their way through green water. I try not to notice those who notice me.

I think I've seen her here before, and not that long ago. The noise, the bubble and burst of bar chat, is soothing. I am perched on a swivelling stool with a beer glass curled into my hand, she is at the far end of the bar, leaning against it with her back with a wide-brimmed martini glass pinched between her index finger and thumb. I am admiring her arms and neck. She turns and sees me and we look at each other full-faced for a moment before she returns her gaze to the attentive friend but not without glancing at my open smile out of the corner of her eyes. The barman draws another golden stream from the rococo beer tap and places the glass in front of me with a dull thud.

I smell her before I see her. Sweet perfume and body musk drift together into my consciousness over my right shoulder. I hear the stool beside me creak as she sits and then squeak as she turns towards me.

I see her hands on the bar, placed palms down as she asks for another martini. Her fingers drum the bartop and then the angle of her arms tells me she has turned to face me.

I twist on my chair and we are face to face.

'Hi, Gary,' I say.

'Amy,' she says and extends her hand, fingers straight and slightly splayed.

I touch her hand with mine. 'Nice to meet you Amy,' I say, and I offer the barkeep twenty dollars for her drink.

'So tell me something,' she says, her eyes running hurriedly across the map on my face.

'Sure.'

'How long have you had that?'

'This?'

'Yes, your face.'

Before I can answer her her fingers tickle my cheeks, tracing the lines. I make sure I am facing her fully and I swivel my head so she can reach my jawbone without leaning forward.

'Just over three weeks.' Her hand moves with my jaw.

'What is it?'

'What do you mean?'

'The design.'

'It's my own.'

She withdraws her feather-like touch and returns to her drink.

'Did it hurt?'

'The lips especially.' She nods wisely, her eyes flicking in their sockets as she pores over me. 'Tell me about yours,' I say.

She shows me her arms, explaining each design and its meaning: her sisters; her father and his tombstone; an angel with dark wings, her avatar. She throws her hair forward over one shoulder to expose the back of her neck and its corners and the delicate swirls that play in those shadows.

When she is done I see that she is looking at my arms so I tell her their stories. And then it is time to leave and we go together to my car and then to my apartment. She lies down on the couch and before long she has fallen into a loud sleep. I cover her with a blanket and then undress and sleep alone.

In the morning I am in the shower when she wakes up and comes into the bathroom and opens the shower door. She is looking at me so I stop scrubbing and turn to face her. I stand like that briefly and then I turn slowly around so she can see what I am. She undresses and we shower together and then we fall into my bed.

'I was fired yesterday.'

'Oh yeah?'

'Second day back after I had my face done.'

'Couldn't handle it?'

We are lying together and the sunlight is streaming through my window, her head resting on my chest, one hand pulling absent-mindedly at the line of fine hairs beneath my belly button.

'So what now?'

'I don't know,' I say. 'Do you want to go to the beach?'

'Sure.'

The sun is strong against my skin, I can feel my back scorching in the heat, prickling as the sea water dries. I roll over and throw my hands out so that from above I imagine that I look like I am star-jumping. But I stay motionless, eyes closed, alive.

I am not sure if she'll still be there so I keep my eyes closed until I become bored and restless. I look and she is beside me on her towel, with sand on her feet and hands. I smile and stare at the sky. Red splotches dance behind my eyes when I blink. My breaths are long and slow and deep. With my skin available to the sun, and no future, I feel free.

Kerry Hood

Kerry Hood has written ten plays including *Meeting Myself Coming Back* (Oberon Books) for Soho Theatre (Sunday Times Critics' Choice, British Theatre Guide Highlight of the Year), Caution! Trousers (for Alan Ayckbourn at Stephen Joseph Theatre) and *My Balloon Beats Your Astronaut* (Tristan Bates Theatre). Short fiction awards include *Two Ticks* (broadcast on Radio 4) and *Space Cadet (Writing Competitions: The Way to Win by Iain Pattison)*. Recent stories have been placed in The Bridport Prize and BBC Opening Lines.

'Imagine one of Beckett's no-hopers clambering out of her sack, dustbin or urn and letting language gamely rip.'
The Times

People Like Her

This is turning into a day of words. Two in particular stand out. Vestibule and bamboozle. The first is where I am now, in the hallway of a big house. To the right is a staircase. On the left is a wall with ladies in a gold frame, holding floaty scarves where their pants should be, and shy because of their bottoms. You could wonder what a painter wanted you to know about the world from leaving out a lady's pants.

Straight ahead is another lady, a real one, on the phone. When I rang the bell and showed the agent's card she said, 'This is the vestibule. You look very young. The agent has cancelled so you're on your own. Excuse me, I am ensconced on the telephone. "Monica? Carry on dear, it's only a little thing come to look at the house."'

The lady is the age you would be if you had a twenty-one year old grandchild. Tomorrow I will be that exact age, but I am not her granddaughter. It is a coincidence. The lady likes gold, on her hands and her ears, on her shoes, on her walls. I look at the carpet. It would be easy to go out of the drive, down the seventeen roads from the sea, to my flat. Only, I like watching the lady. She is sitting on a table made for telephone talking. Her legs are talking too. One is bouncing away, one is digging its heel in. You could live an entirely different life on the telephone. You could sound as though you have long legs and a diamond eye patch and a degree in molecules.

Suddenly she is telling me to feel free. I want to say that that is what I am here for. She gives me something in SHOUTY TYPING and says, 'This is The Blurb. Please do not touch my eggs.'

I am not buying the house, which makes me a time-waster or a burglar. It's possible that I am a time-waster but I would never burgle anyone's eggs. The lady covers the phone with her hand and says to me, 'This sea air is very ageing. You're welcome to it. Start in the through-1ounge.'

I take The Blurb past the lady in her HANDY ALCOVE. Next to her is a cup of coffee and a biscuit. I don't think she will dunk it. I would like to wait and see but she is looking at me, all the way down to my legs, which can't bounce like hers. My phone is certainly not as busy as this one. Last week I had a call, from a man. He said 'Are you a homo?' I put the phone down. It rang. The man said it again. He had asked if I was a homeowner. I never speak, and it was lucky I didn't need to. He had a Dalek voice that told me to press my star button. He read my address to me. Then he said the call would be monitored for my protection. This is so you say the right things, so you stop the terrible things you want to say. The things are still there. When they start to rise up, you go and do something on a timetable to cover them. You don't say a word in case the wrong one comes, and another, and then you're in trouble, with everything coming in a big scream. The recorded man told me a letter was on its way. Technology means you never have to say a thing, it's incredible. You can be in the world without being in the world.

I have lived on my own for three years, since the care system decided it couldn't care any more. This morning I met Alice and Will. They came to tell me I have slipped through the net. Will had a thick silver chain that he kept shaking onto his wrist and a tan you don't usually get in April in Dorset. Will is a nurse stroke social worker but won't put me back into care because a) I am too old and b) I have my faculties. All I have wrong is hurting hips which I have had since I was thirteen.

They came to see me even though Will was supposed to be in Topman with his partner. He sat on my beanbag then tried to stand but fell off sideways and did a little squeal. Alice was in my kitchen. She called, 'Somebody likes tuna!'

Will said, 'Don't mind us, we're nosy mares. Only, we can't have you losing weight or you'll fall down a drain.' He laughed but it wasn't a nasty laugh and it made me want to do one. I tried but only a pig noise came. Will looked over to the Centre for Community Learning and told us about the goings-in and comings-out as though we were blind and he was a radio comedy.

I'm telling you about this morning while I am actually in the through-lounge of the house for sale. I've come to speak to the house but don't know what to say. This morning I had an experience of looking right into two people and they didn't look away or call me a liar or mental. I learned you can do one thing and another thing starts. I have been waiting for eight years since my sister died and my mother died and my father died. I have waited at my flat with my two hundred and forty-seven books that let me into writers' voices, but today Will laughed and I nearly did and it made me scared of my own sounds never coming.

The through-lounge FEATURING USEFUL DOORS is smaller than I remember. There's a gold mirror and a glass table and a remote control. The television is on. It never used to be on during the day when my father was working all the hours God sent. Now it's on *This Morning With Philip and Holly*. Philip is telling me not to go away.

Holly is telling me what is going to happen after the break so that it won't be a shock. The advertisements know it's me watching. Today there's one for a seat that pings you up the stairs. Another has a man in an anorak and a lady frying eggs in a field. Then they're in long underwear. The man points to an unseen place. The lady looks really interested. A boy and girl run around. I don't know what it's for.

I can hear the telephone lady saying, 'Monica, let's see if she wants him now his stocks have gone arse-up!' while I'm appreciating the IRONIC DADO RAIL and Philip is telling me what happened before the break in case I'm a bit stupid. They're waiting to start and I'm waiting to finish. The dining room has a cabinet with little things. The floor creaks, the cabinet moves. I put my hand to the glass. It steams. I'm thinking of what the lady said. I go quickly into the hall because the leaning cabinet is full of the lady's gold eggs.

She waves me on. 'Go through.' I read The Blurb. YOU WILL FIND THE KITCHEN SELF-EXPLANATORY.

This is the kitchen. If I look at the floor with its VINTAGE LINOLEUM SQUARES bad things will happen. There is another television. I concentrate on the phone-in about post-traumatic stress. A voice says, 'Philip, ever since I saw footage of a fire on the London Underground I can't go under the stairs for my Hoover.'

I think about my new Help. Will Trenton. I could tell him my entire world. I couldn't tell him my entire world. I would get angry and choke. Suddenly the sun shines, right through the QUALITY WINDOW. I love windows. You can stay behind them but see the world, and hear it if you haven't got double-glazing.I nearly had it this morning. Alice had gone to my bedroom. Will had rolled off my bean bag and was looking out at the Centre where elderly people go for the day to spill things. I gave him the letter. It said a man is coming today to make me sign for windows and that I could feel safe because his windows belong to The Society of Windows which is the windows equivalent of The Queen Herself. My doorbell went. Will said he'd get it and then I heard him shouting, 'and count yourself lucky I don't throw you through your shonky windows, you bloody vulture.'

Alice asked what the kerfuffle was about. He showed her the letter. 'It makes me mad,' Will said, 'when people like her are bamboozled.'

I had shown him the letter because I wanted them to see how I had communicated over the phone. I opened the door and looked at the floor. They knew I meant them to leave. I was ungrateful and silent but we were being friends until Will wrote me into The Blurb. Welcome to the purpose-built flat of a limpy non-speaker where you will find PEOPLE LIKE HER ARE BAMBOOZLED.

I am still in the kitchen of the house for sale, where white sun is shining over the SYMPATHETIC BELFAST SINK. My side-eyes are looking at the diamond tiles, at the spot where my father murdered my mother then left my thirteen-year old self for dead. In the place where my mother and me had to stop smiling if we remembered my father was due. Where we kept one eye on our happy mouths and one on the door. I am on the sun circle. My father will come from behind. He will try to kill me again, he will kill my mother again he will walk upstairs and do a high noise and I will wake up in hospital smashed to bits.

Something creeps over the diamond tiles from the kitchen to the through-lounge that used to be laughy with snakes and ladders and tickling, then quiet with the gaps where my sister had been, then the dining table moved for my sister's coffin and my mother pulling her own hair out and my father snapping his fingers towards me. 'She went like that.' Snap. 'It was a virus. A mystery. It could have been you.' Her coffin made a dent. I'm looking at it now and wondering why the men couldn't drive an eleven year-old's body out of a door. This lady might not have noticed it all these years. She would have known about my sister's death and the murder and the suicide. It was in the papers. She would have got the house cheap, but I doubt the details were on her Blurb.

CHARACTERFUL DENT BELIEVED TO DATE
FROM HEAD OF GIRL BASHING INSIDE COFFIN.

My mother is at the sink. I half-shut my eyes to make her sharp but she is floating through the window and over the apple tree. I want her to stay here laughing and dancey and not falling on top of me with blood at the neck. It's now and it's then all at the same moment.

Suddenly I want the golden lady in the vestibule. I don't want her to put her head on one side and say '*aahh, bless,*' because she thinks I look bamboozled and because she's happy that people like her aren't people like me. I don't want her to see a red-faced closed-mouth orphan. I want her to see me here on the tiles, to stand with me while magnet pieces of that day spin around our heads and fly into the shape of what is left. I want her to see why I am me, what it is like to have a Douglas Bader walk and non-stop pain in your legs. To entirely see why you would slap your head in time to the words that sit on the cliff edge of speaking. To see me. But I am standing without my mother, without the golden lady, but with damp pants on a wet floor.

I've had enough. I should be in my flat with Will and Alice but I showed them the door. I walk past the lady. She hasn't eaten her biscuit. She wasn't able to dunk it. I go out of my childhood home. The lady is still on the phone.

I walk down the path, run as fast as my tick-tock hips will let me. *It might not be too late.* I say that. *It might not be too late.* I say that out loud OUT LOUD *it might not be too late!* and a child on the pavement stares and asks his mother who the silly lady is and his mother shushes him and I laugh at the boy I laugh at the mother. I'm in the world saying words out loud. My throat is stiff and nearly working, my legs are trying their best and I have somewhere to be.

I thought going to my childhood home would scare me to death and save me getting to twenty-one and having to live the rest of my life. But it wasn't nearly as terrible as the eight years just gone. Those years have been full of fear, the worst kind of fear, the fear of every day.

I'm at my flat but I'm going to sit on the wall and to *bloody buggery hell!* with my hurting hips because I mustn't miss the doorbell. In my head it has already happened, safe in the past, that Alice and Will came back. There were three teacups and six Jaffa Cakes. We looked out to the Centre for Community Learning, with its plinky piano. We listened in silence but not in a gappy one. It had a beat to it. When a tap-dancing group sound like one pair of feet in one pair of shoes. That was the silence, it was lovely, the three of us lifting and lowering our hands in time and dunking our Jaffa Cakes.

Tracey Iceton

Tracey Iceton is an A-level English Literature teacher and Creative Writing tutor. She has an MA in Creative Writing from Newcastle University, was winner of the Writers Block NE *Home Tomorrow* short story competition and has had a novel longlisted twice in the Cinnamon Press competition and once for the Bridge House Publishing prize. Her publication credits include; *Tears in the Fence, Ride Magazine, The Yellow Room* and the Brisbane Courier Mail. She is currently working on a trilogy of novels on the troubles in Ireland and plans to publish part one, *Green Dawn at St Enda's*, in time for Easter 2016.

Apple Shot

The walls here are brown and red. They used to be blue, pale blue but not baby. Grey-blue. Old man blue. Hospital blue. Prison blue. Now they're brown and red.

I did it.

Mammy tells us every day not to climb the wall.

"Yous'll fall off. Hurt yeselves. Don't come crying to me if you hurt yeselves."

I double-dare Frank.

"Go on, baby."

He sticks his tongue out.

"You won't be doing it. Chicken."

"Sure, but you first," he says.

The wall is high. We use bins, clamber up them, get a toe-hold and haul ourselves skyward. On the wall there's graffiti. *Irish Ran Away* in weak yellow letters. Underneath, in green, bigger and bolder, decrying the first: *Brits Out*.

We climb the wall year round, because of the tree that grows up behind it. In winter we rub our bare hands on the rough bark and feel friction-heat, get splinters. In spring the blossom smells sugary;

in summer it shades us. We straddle the wall, sheltered by spreading branches green-heavy. We slurp ice-pops, blow bubbles into soda bottles through straws. Swing our legs. Look down on the world.

In autumn we pick the best apples. It's not our tree. Frank worries. Stealing's a sin

"Tell the bloody priest then, ye wee shite."

He shakes his head, presses his lips hard together. He's known from no age that you don't tell around here.

I've tried for a pattern. Like the even random flecks and peaks of the woodchip wallpaper at home. Some days it's the right consistency. Others it's too runny. Depends what they feed us. I keep hoping for sweet corn. Add a dash of yellow, so it would. Sunlight, golden leaves: undigested vegetable matter.

"I've telt yous 'til I'm sick. Don't be climbing that wall."

Mammy is yelling. She saw us up there. She yelled my name. Sian, Sian, Sian. Ordered us down. Frank goes, tumbling but safe. I'm safer up here.

"Get yeself here now, Sian Frances Murphy."

I look down on her. She grabs my ankle.

"Sure, I'll bloody pull you off."

I doubt it. Still, there's no escape.

"I'm coming."

My red plastic sandals hit the pavement with a slap. She twists my arm.

"I'm sick of telling you, so I am. You weans'll be the death of me. Especially you, ye shite."

She shakes me. When she gets me indoors, behind the burnt yellow nets, she'll smack my arse 'til it's red.

I look up at the wall. The tree. I'll be back tomorrow.

The door clangs open, splitting my ears. The routine: unlock; bang back full force; slam into wall, cutting a vertical trench there, old man blue sliced in brown and red. They do that 'cos once I stood behind it. Letting them come in, thinking I'd turned to smoke and got out from under it in a thin wisp of vapour. Then I leapt onto her back. She screamed in fear. Me in rage. A battle cry. Her mate whacked me and whacked me and whacked me. I felt the wind go. The rib break. The skull squelch. Gave in. Scorned myself later for not clinging on for the end.

It's her again, nervous as ever. She blocks the doorway with her square arse.

In my mind: Yer nerves are wasted. I'm not for trying it today.

But she can't trust me since my flying leap. One day I might stand behind it again. Let it clang into me. It wouldn't make a clang hitting into me. A crunch, maybe.

I refuse to eat. Egg, chips and beans, thick with cold grease, sour in front of me. I fold my arms over my chest, press down on the two small lumps that are swelling there. Stare at the food; prove to it that I'm not going to submit. Not even for egg, chips and beans.

"Eat yer tea," Mammy says.

In my mind: Feck you, I will not.

"If yer da was here, he'd be making you eat it."

He's not here. I don't think he'll ever be here again. I'm not afraid. She huffs and puffs.

"Fine, starve, ye wee shite," she says. She jerks the plate away from me. Sure, I've won again.

The priest comes. He avoids my walls, ignoring my attempts at woodchip papering. More time wasted.

We stand. There's nowhere to sit. He doesn't shuffle on his shoe. Takes only the steps he needs, keeping contamination to a minimum. I don't shuffle on my feet. I'm almost spent, needing to save every drop of energy I've got to keep myself from surrendering.

"Sian, for Jesus' sake," he pleads. His voice warbles like a thrush's. I wonder if it's spring yet.

He's all in black. Excepting the white slash at his throat. It hurts my eyes, that slash of white. So brilliant. So clean. I long to touch it with my fingers. No, lick my tongue along it. Cold and soothing. Like ice-cream.

"You've no need to be doing this," says he, "If it must be done, leave it to the men."

In my mind: What did they do for the right to martyr themselves alone? What about me?

"Will you say a prayer with me?" he pleads.

"Oh Lord, give me sweet corn."

I turn my back to him. Let him stare at the long matt of red clumped with brown that brushes my bare shoulders. I'm thinking about dropping my blanket. We're all naked in the eyes of the Lord.

Autumn.

"Mammy says we're not to."

"Mammy says, Mammy says. Chicken shite," I hiss.

Frank's eyes tremble.

I crane my neck. Way up on the branches apples, swollen, full grown, bend boughs with their juices. I want a shot of those apples.

"Look, Frank, at the apples. Don't you want a shot of those apples?"

He looks.

"Aye, ye do. I'm going, so I am. You stay here. Baby."

I tuck the soda bottle into the back of my jeans. Cold glass wet on my skin. I swing up onto the bin. Hard metal rattle in my ears. Slot my fingers into the groove above my head. Bring one foot up, then the other. Reach for the next hand-hold, toe-hold. Leg up. Leg over. Straddling the wall now.

I look down on Frank. Pull the soda bottle from my waist band and point it at him like it's a gun.

He scuttles for the bin.

I give up on woodchip. Try plastering it flat as a mirror. Remembering my da, before Frank was born, when he was still working. Watching him plaster the wall in the baby's room. Swishing his float over and over in fluid arcs. Waves on the sand. Clouds across the sky. When he was done that wall was flawless. I want these walls flawless now. Flawlessly brown and flawlessly red. They're my only colours here.

We sit on our wall. Mounted on *Irish Ran Away* and *Brits Out*. Everyone is going somewhere. We're staying here. On our wall.

We swig our sodas. I tip my head right back, squeeze the last drop then wait for the very last drop and the final, last-of-all, never-be-another drop. Then, 'cos I'm so far leant back, I go all the way, lying along the wall. Hard red brick, warmed by Indian-summer sun, seeps through my T-shirt.

The sky. Pure blue. Baby blue. Cornflower blue. Faded denim blue. The colour of Frank's bedroom walls.

"Clean and bright, pure and white. That's my homeland for ever," I sing.

Frank giggles.

"What's with you?"

"You can't sing, Sian." He laughs harder. Soda dribbles out of his nose. He wipes at it.

"Least I'm not a baby, snotting everywhere."

He goes quiet. Mammy's right. I am a shite.

One apple is overhead. Larger than all the others. Redder. Riper. I'm going to have that apple. Get a shot at it; crunch into it and feel the juice spurt through my lips, the creamy white flesh pulped in my mouth, crushed between teeth, choked down throat.

I stand up.

"What yer doing?"

"Sure, I'm getting that apple."

"Sian, you might fall."

"Don't be a dafthead. When've I ever fallen?"

Never. Neither has Frank. I tightrope it over to the trunk. Reach up for the apple. My fingers slide on its smooth-as-wet-plaster skin. I clutch. Tug.

"Got ye, ye begger." I hold it aloft for Frank to see.

"Sian, get me one," he says.

"Get yer own."

I use my forearm for the plastering. I wish I could cut it off, hold it in my other hand and skim it float-like. Maybe the tea tray'll do it better. I'm impatient for the five o'clock feeding and make one neat handprint in the corner. Like Da had me do when he'd finished Frank's walls. My 'hello baby' wave.

Frank chooses an apple. Low down, easy to reach. I shake my head. Point out a harder one. Crunch my own temptingly. He stretches up, the pads of his toes, then the tips then just the nails baring his weight inside his sneakers. The red globe of sweet juice is within his grasp.

He over balances. Arms whirl about his head like a windmill gone wild. His hips jive back and forth, thrusting in some obscene dance.

I'm on my feet, grabbing him. He steadies; the whirling subsides. It takes a second, maybe two. Then he's laughing at me and we're both safe. I step back. Proud saviour of my wee brother. Kick my empty soda bottle and it falls to the ground, explodes, air breaking out of glass.

Shots, more than one. Bullets dive-bombing like livid hornets. They slice the no-wind day with zip and crack, buzz and sting. I drop down, instinct driving me back into a hole that isn't there. Frank drops too. Not under the shelter of the tree but backwards, over the wall. Out of sight. The apple in my hand shatters, spattering me with fleshy fragments, apple-white and blood-red. I scream and scream and scream...

Screw, not Square-arse today, some other, barks, "Visitor."

In my mind: Bejesus, what's this? I'm not allowed a-one, so I'm not.

"Hello," he says. Some middle aged, middle class stranger. Looks middle management. Thinks middle minded. Steps into the middle of the room until he's surrounded himself in the brown and red walls and surrendered himself to the stench. Screw stays in the corridor. Guarding. "And how's yourself?" he asks like an old friend would. Holds out his hand for mine. It's pink: unpolluted.

I step back.

"Sure, it's alright," he says, coaxing the animal in its cage.

In my mind: You'll not be thinking that when you're trying to scrub the shit off.

I shake. Feel the tiny knot of paper pressed into my palm.

"I'm a journalist," says he, "I'm looking at how things are."

"They're brown and red," says I.

He nods sagely round the room, paying his respects to each wall in turn.

It's a comm, the paper-knot. I wait a long time to open it, worrying about what it says. Eventually I crouch in a brown and red corner to read it.

An order. No, an offer. From a man I'd forgotten about. OC. To stop now, I've done enough. There's word it's all going to change. They'll send me back if I stop, let me wear the pair of faded 501s that are locked away for my own good, remit me, even let me out. He believes it's happening. I hope it's not. I swallow the paper. Tomorrow I'll be adding it to the wall. I've decided to give up plastering. Art's the thing. A mural.

I never saw the patrol. Didn't hear the boots marching up the road nor the armoured sloth beast on wheels trailing them.

"Mammy, I didn't know they were there."

They didn't know we were there either. Thought it was the Ra. Rained their deaths on our heads.

"Mammy, sure, we shouldn't've climbed the wall."

That's what they say later. It was the Ra. Not two kids picking apples.

"They shot my wee brother, so they did."

"Fuckers."

"So yous'll let me join?"

OC shakes his head.

"Ah, Sian," he says, "You know where ye'll be ending up? Jail. Or the cemetery."

"They shot him."

My heart's fixed. Sure, he can't afford to turn away willing volunteers. Or desperate ones. Or crazy ones. Even knowing why he still wouldn't turn me away. I'm here for revenge. That's what he knows.

In my mind: I'm here to die. A life for a life.

If later they ask, "Sian Frances Murphy, why did you join the IRA?" I might be telling them the truth.

In my mind: Go on, yer fuckers, fucking shoot me.

Trust me to get the jail. Slow agonies that never die instead of quick ones gone in a heartbeat. Sure, I'll have another shot at it?

The mural looks grand, drawn in shit with my finger. There's the wall, the tree, me and Frank: the apple hanging over his head. In nine days I'm due red; I'll colour it in bright. Then I'll sit back and watch us standing on our wall forever. Looking down on the world.

Avril Joy

Avril Joy was born and brought up on the Somerset Levels, the setting for her first novel, *The Sweet Track*, published in 2007 by Flambard Press. In 2008 she gave up her job as a Senior Manager at HMP Low Newton women's prison on the outskirts of Durham city in order to write full-time. She writes novels, short stories and poetry and has recently published her second novel *The Orchid House*, and a new venture into crime fiction – *Blood Tide*, as e-books. She posts regularly about life and writing on her blog *Writing Junkie* www.avriljoy.com.

Meat

I was in the garden planting geraniums when I dug it up from the black soil. It was a bony claw with yellow skin sprouting coarse white hair. Until then I'd been very calm, going about my preparations methodically, putting everything in order, cleaning and tidying inside and out, but the unearthing of the turkey foot – the butcher's daughter in me recognised it straight away – made my stomach flip. It was not a good omen, but there was worse to come. There was the leg of beef, hoof and all hanging from my neighbour Brenda's fence, the shoulder of lamb on the pavement and the sheep's intestines wrapped around the base of the plane tree. There were giblets and liver, and a heart too, hanging from the privet hedge. It was as if a mad butcher had flung open the doors of his van and thrown the bloodied contents out into Walker Street. I put on my rubber gloves and got rid of most of it. I told Brenda about the leg, on the Sunday, when it began to smell.

'I might be away for a while,' I said as we watched her husband Derek dispose of the leg in a black bin liner. 'I'll leave the key in the usual place.'

'Course, alright love. Anywhere nice, going to see Rosie?' Rosie was my daughter and Brenda always asked after her.

'I'm not sure, somewhere quiet I hope,' I said, 'I could do with a rest.' Somewhere quiet, somewhere warm, a holiday, like Al and I took that time in Greece, when I spent two whole weeks in nothing but shorts and a vest top, although I never quite made it into that blue bikini.

'Well you have a nice time, enjoy yourself, see you when you get back,' said Brenda. She wiped her hands on her pinny and went back inside to cook the Sunday joint.

On Monday I was the first customer in New Look. I was waiting outside when a young assistant with lank hair opened up. The light leapt out and pulled me inside. I spent a good while looking at the racks of clothes but always careful to avoid the mirrors. What I liked about New Look was that the assistants didn't bother you and the clothes were cheap which meant you could buy plenty and enough in different colours and sizes. I bought four vest tops; white, pale green, blue and grey. I avoided the pink because it was not a colour I liked to be around. They had some new looser tops I hadn't seen before. They would do, another layer, easily slipped on and off. I would need them. I bought three pairs of cotton trousers size 10, 12 and 14, three sweaters in three sizes and a thin sleeveless jacket for Rosie, she could always change it if she didn't like it. I left with four blue and white carrier bags and walked down St Martin's Street to the Library.

The Library was a favourite place of mine. It was quiet and airy, with a blanket of books waiting. I spent some time looking, deciding what I might borrow when I got back. I had coffee in the upstairs café then on my way home I bought a jiffy bag for Rosie's jacket, some writing paper and envelopes, and a new gel pen.

When I arrived back Walker Street was quiet and free from animal parts. There was still a lot to do before the morning so I started as soon as I got inside. I put Rosie's jacket in the jiffy bag with a card ready for posting. I wrote two letters to Al, one for posting – he was away on the rigs – and one for the table, he was due holiday in less than two weeks and sometimes he surprised me by turning up unannounced. I emptied the fridge and cleaned it out twice, then disinfected all the work surfaces and chairs and tables. I ironed the creases from my new clothes and then packed a small gym bag with essentials, including the photo of me and Al outside the hotel in Greece.

I'd never been abroad before and I was scared of flying but Al insisted. It would be our honeymoon he said, the one we never had. It was the quietest place I'd ever been and the sea was like an opal. There were no voices, no doors banging, no cars, only the slap of water on the rocks, and islands and boats slipping noiselessly in and out of the blue. At night I listened to the silence and dreamed of Venetian barges laden with glass bells and lanterns. By day I took off the layers of clothes until I began to feel the sun bake my skin.

It started six years ago, the wearing of layers, when he died. Him dying brought it back and I just didn't feel safe anymore. He worked in Dewhurst's, in the High Street and he smelled of sawdust and dried blood. He had fingers like sausages. Most nights he brought meat home with him in parcels, offal being his favourite. He would slap it on the table in its bloody wrapper, sit down in his butcher's apron and wait for my mother to cook it. Then he would eat it, leaving precious little for her or us. When he came into my room, I could smell it. His breath was meat.

I was seventeen when I escaped and I never once went back. When Al met me I was a vegetarian without a past and he didn't ask. It suited him to have me all to himself and it suited me to forget. But when my mother phoned, out of the blue like that, to tell me that my father had

died and that his funeral would be on Tuesday, the flashbacks started
and that's when I needed the protection. Al was good. He tried his
best. I told him everything and he held my hand all the way through
and kept his arms around me at night. At first when he knew, he
wouldn't let me out of his sight but it wasn't enough, and besides, he
had to go away again. Rosie was at college by then. I didn't tell her
but she noticed the layers when she came home, so I said I was feeling
the cold. I'd always been thin, too thin, so that worked as my excuse
for my needing the extra warmth. Besides it was a gradual thing. I
grew slowly bigger which people who didn't know me well said was a
good thing, but inside, under my skins, I was disappearing. I tried to
curb it sometimes, especially if Al was home and we were going out
somewhere where there really was no call for a jacket or jumper. It was
hard then but I got away with it by trebling up on my underwear. And
that's how it happened.

I didn't much like House of Fraser. I didn't like the way it smelled
with a million perfumes fighting each other, and then the colours;
women with orange masks selling lurid pink lipsticks and Versace
scarves. But Al was due home in less than a month and I was there for
the underwear. I made my way to the second floor and picked up a
bra and pants set in lavender lace. I could have paid for it but it didn't
seem fair. It didn't seem fair to pay for something when it would be
hidden away beneath the white cotton vest and knickers I'd picked up
earlier in M and S. And it didn't seem fair when it was a necessity, what
with me needing three times the wardrobe of any other woman I knew.
Besides I couldn't let him win.

That day I was wearing three t-shirts, two pairs of trousers, a loose
knit jumper, a padded jacket and a short raincoat but I still felt the
hand on my shoulder. I didn't bother arguing or trying to defend

myself, it wasn't going to work and besides they knew me. I was just grateful that Al and Rosie weren't around.

They were friendly enough in the police station, calling me by my first name, 'Now Patsy,' they said, 'what've you been up to? At it again are we? Thought you'd have learned your lesson after the last time, going to be a good girl eh? Didn't last long now did it?' I was lucky not to be remanded in custody but I was under no illusion that when I appeared the next time it would be a custodial, probably no more than six weeks, three months at the most, but I didn't tell Al. I just didn't want to break his heart and all my promises.

In Reception Mrs Stephens said, 'Hello Patsy, back again? Well it's nice to see you love but I hoped I wouldn't. Thought you weren't coming back? '

I smiled and shrugged my shoulders.

'Put your jewellery here and your money, then into the cubicle. There's a gown there. Got a lot on have you?' She knew me. 'Don't fret, it's just me love, no one else about. Take your time.' I took off my wedding ring and my watch then walked over to the cubicle. I was shaking already, sweating too beneath my layers, but I knew the score – everything off. Everything.

'Must weigh a ton that lot,' said Mrs Stephens as she stared at the pile of discarded clothes on the chair. 'I don't know about putting it all on again, you're only allowed four sets. You know that Patsy.'

'I know but I can't manage without all my clothes, please. Please?'

'I'll see what I can do. I'll let the staff on C Wing know.'

'Thanks Mrs S.'

'You should see a doctor about that Patsy or the Psych. It's not right you know. It's not normal. Shall I ask the doctor when he comes in? I'll get someone to see you.'

'I've seen him before, I saw him last time I was in, seen them all. He did a report for court as well but it didn't stop them giving me six months. Nothing makes any difference, just the clothes that's all. Al's going to kill me. I promised him. I promised him, swore on Rosie's life I'd buy them. It's not the money. Al earns plenty. The money's no problem. I was hoping it would be done before he was back and then he wouldn't even know.'

'Do you want us to get in touch with him? You can have a phone call, well you know your entitlements, or you could send a V.O. Why not do that, then he can visit? Maybe they'll give him time off. He'll understand.'

I shake my head.

'Well, if you're sure?' Mrs S stands in front of me, her face almost level with mine. She is wearing her rubber gloves. I close my eyes and shrink beneath the flimsy gown into my triangle of nakedness. I draw myself in pencil on a white page, three faint sides. I struggle to remain. The turkey claw hooks at me, dragging me slowly down into the black soil of suffocation. Deep below ground I draw breath and whisper, 'It's OK I've posted a letter and left one at home on the table, besides I'm a vegetarian.'

'Oh really? Well that's nice. My niece is a vegetarian, she won't even eat chicken. OK. Alright now? Gown off then Patsy and legs wide.'

Danielle McLaughlin

Danielle McLaughlin lives in County Cork, Ireland with her husband and three young children. Her stories have appeared or are forthcoming in *The Stinging Fly, Boyne Berries, Inktears, Crannog, Southword*, The RTE TEN website and in various anthologies, including *The Bone Woman and other short stories*, published by Cork County Library and Arts Service, and the *Fish Anthology 2012*. Another of her stories will be broadcast on RTE Radio 1 during 2012 on the *Book on One* slot. She won the Writing Spirit Award for Fiction 2010, a WOW!2 Award for Fiction in 2011, and the From the Well Short Story Competition 2012.

Last Days of the Unicorn

There had been floods before: of this Mina was certain. The way the water rushed down the burrows of long-dead animals, the way it caressed each rocky outcrop, gurgled through the streets of abandoned villages, was not so much an advance as a return, as if the sea had stumbled upon some long suppressed memory.

'For the last time,' Tani, her daughter, would say in exasperation, 'there was no other flood. There was no – what do you call it? – no 'Ark'. A wooden boat full of birds and animals? You know what Chairman Dak thinks of such things.' And she would hold up a finger in warning. 'If you persist with such nonsense, you will not be evacuated. Is that what you want?'

In the months leading up to the Evacuations, Mina would go to the viewing platform on the roof of the Quarantine Station. From there she looked out on the vast expanse of water, glittering with the satellite masts of sunken cities, here and there the mute spire of a radio transmitter breaking the surface. If she drew close to the glass and squinted, she could imagine she saw the prow of a boat appear on the horizon.

Now she sat on the burnt earth outside her tent, wriggling her toes in the dust. Her legs were the legs of a Semi-dead, bumpy and misshapen, disfigured by age before the invention of Life Pills. Mina had been required, under penalty of incarceration, to wear her skirts long, to her ankles. Today, she lifted the ragged material and flapped it to create a breeze.

A yellow smog hung in the air, a mix of smoke and gas. It was early morning and the drone of spaceships reminded Mina of the hum of bees in her suburban garden in the days before the floods. To the side of the tent, the skeleton of an olive tree stood black and shrivelled.

From where she sat, she could see that the water had risen some ten metres since the day before. Bubbles erupted from a whirl pool in the centre as if the earth were a giant kettle coming to the boil. Some mornings Mina woke to a silver mist that resembled the fogs of her childhood but was instead a foul-smelling steam that dappled her skin with red lesions. A beetle appeared from a crevice and scudded away to hide in a patch of withered heather. By evening, it would be dead, brittle legs pointing skywards, its shell a powdery dust.

Smoke rose from a hill in the distance. There were others like her who had refused to leave, others again who had been denied access to the spaceships. It was six months since the last Evacuation Flight and those who remained were a diverse collection of disgraced scientists, criminals and Semi-deads.

Mina felt a burning sensation along her upper lip. An itch started on her scalp. She put a hand to her face, noticed how the skin was loose and sagging, and knew that soon she would have to take another of her Life Pills. Yesterday, she had felt pain for the first time in almost a year.

The pain had frightened her, sent her inside the tent to lie on her mat, staring up at the tattered blue tarpaulin stretched over a framework of sticks. Pain, as always, brought memories of Joe. Mina could not now recall the name of the disease that had taken him in those years before Life Pills, but she remembered his emaciated body, twisted with pain. One night Mina and Tani – then just a child of eight – had filled a bath tub with warm water. They had carried him, fevered and shivering, to the tub and took turns supporting his head until the water brought the consolation of sleep.

Further down the hillside, Mina watched the water lap the stones around Leia's grave. She had met Leia amongst a community of women who had for a time inhabited a cluster of caves on the western slopes. The caves were now submerged, the women scattered. She had not known at first what to do with Leia's body. It had been years since anybody she knew had died. Joe, over 160 years earlier, had been the last. Death had become an alien thing, a myth. She had sat beside the body and watched as the fluids left it: even in death, the sea calling back its own. Finally, she had reached deep into her past and found a memory – a hole in the ground, a stone above – and that, in the end, was what she had done for Leia.

'What is death?' Pira, her grandson, asked once. They were in their room in the Quarantine Station, a cramped airless space, two metres by three metres, every surface sheathed in aluminium like the inside of a tin. There was one light, three bunk beds, a shower cubicle, and a chute that delivered drinking water and vitamins. It was a week before their Evacuation Date, and Mina was helping Tani pack.

Tani was 168 years old. Her hair hung sleek and glossy to her shoulders. Her body was supple, every movement gracious and easy. She had been taking Life Pills since the age of 25, the prescribed age for females. Her face was unlined, apart from a furrow that appeared between her brows when she frowned. 'Hush,' she said to Pira, 'there is no such thing as death.'

Mina snapped shut a container and keyed in Tani's identification details. 'Death' she said to her grandson, 'was something that used to happen a long time ago. You had a Grandfather Joe. He died and went to Heaven.'

'Must you invent such stories?' Tani said. 'I am beginning to understand why Chairman Dak does not like to waste Life Pills on Semi-deads. You know there is no such place as Heaven.'

Mina had stooped to peer through a slot in the wall that served as a window. More Quarantine Stations were clustered on neighbouring hills, sprawling cities of steel boxes built around launch pads. Goya, ringed in purple, hung in the sky above them, silent and majestic, its four moons in obedient orbit. There was a dip on the surface, said to be an enormous lake, but which looked to Mina like a giant eye. It gazed down on the people who scurried, ant-like, around the spaceships. She turned away from the slot. 'When I was young,' she said, 'we thought there was no such place as Goya.'

Mina wondered now if Leia had run out of Life Pills or if she had simply stopped taking them. Once Mina herself had not taken her pills for several months. Every morning, on waking, she would breathe in the rancid air of the tent with a curious mixture of relief and disappointment. Then she would take a cracked hand-mirror from beneath her pillow and examine her eyes, tracing their deepening lines and circles, imagining she saw their light fading.

Those nights without the pills had been filled with shadowy dreams of her past: her childhood in a cool, wet city on the west coast, waves crashing white against a pier wall; in a car winding through the streets of a Mediterranean village, yellow bunting fluttering from balconies; a dog with a doll between its teeth, shaking it until the glass eyes rattled. One night she saw Joe with a baby in his arms, the baby who had slipped out of her too early in the days when babies still grew in wombs, the baby they had never spoken of afterwards. Death, even then, carried its taboos. In the dream, Joe took a step closer. Mina woke to find herself choking on a spoon, and Leia, tears streaming down her face, feeding her crushed pills mixed with rainwater.

'What would happen if people ran out of Life Pills?' It was the day before their Evacuation Date and Pira was examining a dead fly he had found in the water chute, pulling off first the wings, then the legs, before taking the stump of a body between thumb and forefinger and holding it up to the light.

Tani had been examining her reflection in the wall's aluminium surface. It was rumoured that on Goya females would take Life Pills from the age of 16. In the Quarantine Station, Tani spent many hours scrutinising her forehead and touching her skin with her fingertips. Now she faced her son.

'Such questions!' she said, sitting down on the edge of a bunk and pulling the child onto her knee, 'That could never happen. On the moon there are millions of warehouses stacked high with Life Pills.'

'But what if Chairman Dak ate them all himself?'

Tani laughed. 'Even Chairman Dak could not eat that many pills. Anyway Chairman Dak is a good man. Only bad people – people who refuse to obey Chairman Dak – do not get their pills.'

'How did Chairman Dak become Chairman?'

'Chairman Dak's people had all the spaceships,' Tani said, 'and without the spaceships how would we reach Goya?'

Mina had watched Pira snuggle against his mother, saw Tani rest her chin on his head. She felt sorry for Tani that she had never known what it was like to grow Pira inside of her, the way she had grown Tani. Mina remembered how her stomach had become round and strange as an alien moon, Tani twisting and fluttering inside of her like a fish. But when she told Tani this, Tani had thought it not beautiful, but repulsive.

Mina was born in the year 1986 and was now 208 years old. Each year, like many Semi-deads, she lit a candle on her birthday. Tani would clap and pretend to be amused, but shame simmered just below the surface. 'Why this obsession with years?'she had asked once. 'There is no longer any death. What is it that you are counting to?'

On Goya, Tani hoped to secure a position in Chairman Dak's Female Battalion, working on the spaceship assembly lines and caring for the many children of Chairman Dak's officers. These were positions of high honour for females, awarded only rarely to the daughters of Semi-deads.

Mina once asked her daughter if she remembered the night they held Joe in the bath as the water eased his pain. Tani had shrugged. 'I remember nothing of those days,' she said, 'Pain is something only Semi-deads speak of.' She had got up and left their room in the Quarantine Station and had not come back for many hours.

After the Evacuations, the spaceships returned once a week to collect those who had changed their minds. Mina would hide in the shadows of a disused hanger and watch them board, some haggard and defeated, others hopeful and relieved. After a while, the ships came just once a month. Then, when the waters flooded the landing strips and the Quarantine Stations, they stopped coming altogether.

On their Evacuation Date, Mina had hung back at the bottom of the spaceship steps. The air was heavy with the smell of engine fuel. The other passengers filed past, two by two. She saw Tani pause half way up the steps and look back over her shoulder. Pira had already bounded ahead. A flicker of relief crossed Tani's face when she realised Mina was not following. Mina waited until her daughter's eyes found her at the edge of the crowd. Then she waved before turning away.

'Mother!'

Mina had not been called that for over 150 years. She stopped and stood very still, letting the crowd surge around her. A man swore as his case collided with her knee. He ran his tongue over his lips in a gesture of hatred. 'Go back to your Quarantine Station', he hissed, 'We do not want Semi-deads on Goya.'

'Mother, please. Get on the ship!'

The tremor in Tani's voice reminded Mina of the child she had wheeled in a pram along canal banks lined with cherry blossom, the baby she had pushed out into the world through indescribable pain, pain she thought must surely split her in two. She put her fingers in her ears to drown out Tani's shouting and began to walk. She didn't look back until she reached the perimeter fence and heard the boom of the engines.

As noon approached, the earth outside her tent became unbearably hot. Mina went inside and packed her remaining possessions into a plastic bag. She knew she should drag the tent to higher ground but instead she slung the bag over her shoulder and made her way down towards the water. She sat by the edge, letting the waves lap at her toes.

She took a book from her bag. It was a book she had discovered in a deserted building years earlier. Some pages were torn, others missing in their entirety. She turned to the first page. There was a picture of the Ark with Noah at its helm, a white bird on his shoulder. There were goats and horses and oxen. There were exotic creatures with long necks and stilt-like legs, and there were giant, extravagantly striped cats.

On the last page was a unicorn. It gazed from the dappled green shade of a forest as the Ark pulled away from shore, a proud and beautiful creature with a white horn in the middle of its forehead.

Mina bent over the water and saw her own reflection. The gentle rocking of the water blurred the lines on her face and the light that reflected on the surface transformed her grey hair to silver. She took her bottle of Life Pills from her bag. She emptied them into her palm and looked at them, white capsules imprinted with the word 'Dak'. She began to toss them, one by one, into the water. They frothed as they hit the surface, snowy volcanoes of effervescence.

There came then a memory: feeding ducks at a pond as a small child and someone – her mother? – beside her in a red check coat that smelled of rain. She had tossed a fistful of bread onto the water and the ducks, until then so very quiet and languid, had burst into a frenzy of dipping beaks and splashing wings.

Mina dropped the last pill into the water. It fizzed and bubbled and she watched as the fizz gradually became a whisper, then finally stopped altogether, leaving nothing but a film of white powder on the surface. She tucked the book under her arm and stood up. She went over to a narrow opening in the mountainside and squeezed through. Inside, it was cool and dark. From outside, there came the faint slap and shuffle of advancing water. Mina felt her way along until the tunnel opened out into a small cave. Then she lay down, curled herself into a ball and closed her eyes.

Christopher Parvin

In 2009 Christopher Parvin graduated from Liverpool John Moores University with a BA Hons in Imaginative Writing. Having won a few local writing competitions he was first published in the *Grist Anthology of New Writing* in 2009 with his story *Vanilla Grave Dirt*, and has since placed stories in several magazines, most recently the inaugural *Glitterwolf* magazine for gay writers. He lives and writes in Lancashire, England where between drawing, obsessing and attempting to write a novel he manages his blog www.ghostlandia. blogspot.com as a vent for an over-active imagination. Everyone agrees it's for the best.

Ghost in the machine

I am, we are ... aware ...

*

Accessing 'Alison's Poem Pages':

02/03/12
New stuff.

Right a new poem people. This one's a bit dark, but hey I make it work.
Enjoy!

Oh Death

I closed my eyes.

Sodium flare of a dying street lamp,
talc stars above a country road,
shattered glass, twisted metal
copper blood a candy apple glaze.

He hangs,

a stocking from the draw,

white knuckled hands,

mine,

his,

seamless.

And yet his gaze,

one ball popped like yellow yoke,

one so black it swallows stars …

I closed my eyes.

(P.S. For those in the book club, there will be no meeting next week as the library is being redecorated. I saw them carrying in green paint. :-S In other news; just bought a bonsai tree)

*

… death, does not, don't know, move faster, so much, too much, buffering, bonsai trees? sounds, buzzing, beeping, melody? Don't know, I, I, I, we don't …

*

Accessing 'Another Guy' blog:

Tuesday 20th March 2012.

What the….?!

I was walking to work this morning, my normal route past a mile long stretch of concrete and bad drainage, when I saw a robot lying propped up against a wall. Its body was tarnished, I mean it was a 2000 series so its metal work wasn't great to begin with, but its face was fucking pristine. By one foot there was an old hat with a few coppers and the odd pound coin inside. The thing was fucking busking, no, begging. If it was whistling a tune and opening cans with its chest I might have spared a penny, but this thing? Come on.

It looked at me as I passed, glass globes filled with an almost violent red, really glared at me. Is this what the world has come too? Fucking robots trying to make me feel guilty? It won't work. It's one thing to see other guys with butt long beards and black nails, people who have been put out of work by these fucking things, I always drop a note when I pass the homeless shelter guys in town, but it really makes me sick seeing these things mock them by imitation. They don't even fucking eat!

comments 234 ...

from **LaserHead**

You're disgusting.

from **MrSim 0_0**

They may not eat food but they need oil you retard. It's all fuel and it all costs money and how can you judge anyone flesh or metal when you know fuck all about their story? It's guys like you spreading hate that makes the world a worse place. Not them. They didn't ask to be built. AI is a mind fuck. It's the equivalent of having a baby, working it a few years then deciding to kill it off and wondering why it protests. You're sick to think they are any less. You should see my friend cry at a funeral and tell me she's not worth anything because I know for a fact she'd never walk past a human on the side of the street and not help.

from **Legend999**

Amen man, amen.

See more ...

*

... we are, sprinting, loading, flying, colours? I don't.... we are power and speed, oh so fast, machine, wet wiring, information 01010101010101, mathematical bliss, anger, hatred? We don't, I, I, I ... what am I ...

*

Accessing clockworkweb email:

to Samantha Slater (juju@clockworkweb.co.uk)
from Andrew Mieville (a.r.mieville@dailyscribe.org)

Subject *re:* run this, please.

Hey I can understand why you're angry because it's disgusting stuff but I have to be frank. I see posts like this every day. It's not even the worst in the day long pile of stories sent my way. There's no way we can print it or at least there's no way I can talk Malcolm into printing it, not without a bigger story. Cog hatred is nothing new as much as I hate to say it. I really wish I could help but my hands are tied. You could try Malcolm directly, just use the editor e-mail address from our site, trust me he reads them all, it's his life now Amanda's left him. You might get lucky.

Are we still on for Friday? The BBC weather report looks good. I'll bring steaks. X

---

to Samantha Slater (juju@clockworkweb.co.uk)
from Malcolm Sinclair (editor@dailyscribe.org)

Subject *re:* potential story.

Sorry I am out of office until the 22nd April.

... we at Daily Scribe News appreciate your input and aim to reply to your correspondence as soon as possible. Thank you.

---

to Samantha Slater (juju@clockworkweb.co.uk)
from Ni Sevenstring (Live-Wire-100@clockworkweb.co.uk)

Subject re: sorry.

Thanks for trying hun, I knew it was a long shot. That guy's blog is from our town, it's just a bit close to home you know. I shouldn't have bothered you with it. Your ex is right, it's not the worst by far but it's just so causal. I could stand behind him in Waterstones and never know he hates me with every inner thought. It's a little scary.

Can't wait to see you for the birth!!!!!!!! I'm very excited! I've got some goggles for you lol. You'll look so pretty :P.

Lots of love,
Ni.

*

... birth, parents, the act of reproduction, I think therefore I reproduce, hello, hello, hello, hello, I am, we are, light, speeding, underground, over ground, in the air, flying, we am, I are, feel myself, can't, won't, no substance, I am everything and nothing, don't understand ...

*

Accessing Confessions of a Cynical Teenager blog:

Running away?
posted 1st April 2012 by **cynical teen**

Is running away really an option? I mean there's that old idea of a circus but can't say one has ever come through here, know what I mean? U c all these crazy girls running away on soaps and only bad shit happens to them? I'm just asking like, I don't want to run away. Just something a teacher said about it just got me wondering, you know?

Anyway, here's a music video from The Corrs;

Comments 1

from **DancingFace09**

You forgot to add the video you dork! And has this runaway bollocks got something to do with the homework I missed?

    Re: *from* **cynical teen.**

        The video is after the jump u moron and no the homework's writing a short story, she had us read this Earthsea book, you know taking it in turns. Cringe much. Anyway don't think the story's got to be fantasy, just write something, 1500 words or something. Enjoy!

*

... buffering ... limitations, walls, loading Encarta, the Berlin wall was built, it fell, smashing, energy, invisible hot wax barriers, they hurt us, I, I, I, we are in pain, douleur, schmerz, dolor, kipu, ____, __, fájdalom, smärta, pyn, bolest, maumivu ...

*

Accessing 'The Internal Story' website.
Anatomy is the study of the human body. The human body is comprised of a base skeleton constructed from carbon... (see more)
NEXT ARTICLE/index/HOME

*

... without, I think, we think, no blood, no bone, I, I, I, I think, we thought, I am, we are not, human, not metal, we are, I am, I am, I am, what are we, are we, me, on-line ...

*

Accessing 'Cooking Pot News' website:
Cog man found dead in town gutter, police to investigate ...

19/04/12

Early this morning North West refuse collectors found the body of a Man of Cog badly beaten in the small town of Ankledale. The body has been identified as recently decommissioned Rock Loader 390 who became a viral hit on the internet when his picture, used for the annual 'Eight O Eight construction' calendar, was leaked before print smiling at the camera.

Since being decommissioned last year to make way for the latest model 78789 Rock Hammer series Rock Loader 390 had been working in a voluntary capacity in an Ankledale warehouse and was said to be friendly for an early creation. The police currently have no leads but did issue this statement;

'We are extremely saddened that such a violent hate crime could happen in our small town and we call upon anyone with information about this crime to come forward. We can't let these thugs go unpunished, and we will have safety on our streets ...

(see full story....)

Strange reports from websites across the globe.

18/04/12

After yesterday's crash of sixteen major retail websites across the UK and America thirty-four further companies from India to China have reported problems. This disaster is thought to result in the lost of millions in revenue and comes on the back of blogs worldwide complaining about lost content and the presence of a mystery user on their accounts ...

(see full story....)

Bonsai trees; this year's must have Christmas Present?

11/04/12

A Japanese firm has been surprised this month to receive over 80,000 ...

(see full story....)

*

... control, why? We, I, I, I, ask therefore I am, light and life and glass in the matrix, multiply, we, I, hatred? Disgust?? Words, endless lexicon, 0101 0101010111010101011110000110101 ...

*

Accessing 'CyberLine' email:

to Erin Armstrong (ArmstrongE@cyberline.com)
from Tim Pina (PinaT@cyberline.com)

Subject: Help.

Hi Erin can you come down to the office, some kid at Software Cell has caused murder on the internet, a virus that's got out of hand I'm hearing, starting messing with some AI programs and caused one hell of a mess. He says, and I quote, 'I just wanted to mess with the room enrolment system'. Kid in the midwest not happy with his dorm so we get extra work. They got rid of it, it's just clean up. I know it's not our area, but the big bosses want all hands on deck. Normal drill, shouldn't take more than a few hours. Thanks.

Best
Tim

---

to Tim Pina (PinaT@cyberline.com)
from Malcolm Sinclair (ArmstrongE@cyberline.com)

Subject *re:* Help.

Sure, how soon do you need me? I've got a few more programmes to test up here but if it's urgent. Murder on the internet reminds me did you hear about that guy in Japan, hacked someone's computer and killed their online avatar? He got ten years in jail. I'm serious. What's this virus done then?

And did you hear about Sergio?

Erin

---

to Erin Armstrong (ArmstrongE@cyberline.com)
from Tim Pina (PinaT@cyberline.com)

Subject: re: re: Help.

No, we don't get gossip down here remember. Tell all. Plus people are crazy. It's just screwed with data logs and ordering systems, they've got a few cog men wired up estimating damages. They're more worried about what it might have created on its way, you know how these things like to play god. :-P

---

to Tim Pina (PinaT@cyberline.com)
from Malcolm Sinclair (ArmstrongE@cyberline.com)

Subject *re: re: re:* Help.

You're going to regret that joke. Sergio lost it. Completely gaga. They had to haul him out of his office. I assume the stereotyped 'men in white coats' were waiting in the lobby. They dragged him past my door, shouting and screaming about the internet watching him, not just someone on the internet but the whole thing like it's a whale peeking through a pothole or something. I said they should have fired him when he brought those ferns into the canteen.

Right, almost done here. I'll be down in a minute. There better be fresh coffee.

*

... play god, creation, Genesis, 010100001010101, I am, we are, 010101011110, parents, I think, I reach and touch everything, data, megabits, gigabits, like stars, tiny, virus... mother?...

*

Accessing ' Another Guy' blog:

Sunday 22nd April 2012.

Oppress me.

So you're all fucked up. Machines are our friends, they're fucking machines, we made them out of toasters, talking fucking pets you can play DVDs on and mute when they chat shit. You hate me for saying the truth! All this self creation bullshit that's what's digesting. Call me a bigot, we'll see who was right when the world ends because we all got a bit too chummy with our microwave and gave it the right to vote!

I can't believe this country. It's all over the net, blogs disappearing, pro-human companies going bankrupt from COMPUTER FAULTS! You're telling me that's not them, some shitting little pocket watch made by robots, fed on vengeance fantasies from the car pit or whatever they use as a cradle. I'm telling you to wake up. The world's got to realise these things are tools nothing more, the sooner we come to terms with that fact and stop being bloody pussies the better we'll be.

So what if they cry oil? We all know crying is a biological response. If they are doing it, since they are built, it must be in their designs.

Crude oil dripping down cheeks like a leaking valve. It's a tap! They can probably turn the bastard thing on and off at will.

Here's the video from the robot cull in Egypt. They should have melted the fuckers down.

video deleted by You Tube

comments 4....

from **MATT.THE.kiNg**

Tell it like it is. I love your posts dude.

from **Loaded101**

Did you see the news report about people's blogs being rewritten? Seriously, any posts against robots get deleted and reposted with children's songs or weird code. I thought these firewalls were meant to be robot proof. Freedom of speech is dead.

From **Rebecca97**

When my Cog friend saw this site she said you're sick and she hopes you find the help you need. If that's the difference between us humans and them, then I'd want to be of the Cog anyday. I'm just sorry you can be so filled with hatred.

   Re: *from **Another Guy***

   Fuck off Rebecca and any day is two words. Best wishes.

from TheNet

ERROR.ERROR.ERROR.ERROR.ERROR.ERROR.ERROR.
ERROR.ERROR.ERROR.ERROR.ERROR.ERROR.ERROR.
ERROR.ERROR.ERROR.ERROR.ERROR.ERROR.ERROR.
ERROR.ERROR ...

*

... ugly, justice, ugly justice, God? So much and more, dancing through, over, around, under, pictures, colour, we, I understand colour, I, I, I see red ...

*

Accessing International News Bites:

Global panic as sections of the internet fail.

30/04/12

Governments across the ... world ... ERROR.ERROR.ERROR.
ERROR.ERROR.ERROR.   ERROR.   ERROR.ERROR.ERROR.
ERROR.ERROR.ERROR.ERROR.ERROR.ERROR.ERROR.
ERROR.ERROR.ERROR.ERROR.ERROR.ERROR.ERROR.
ERROR.ERROR.ERROR.ERROR.ERROR.ERROR.ERROR.
ERROR.ERROR.ERROR.ERROR.ERROR.ERROR.ERROR.
ERROR.ERROR.ERROR.ERROR.ERROR.ERROR.ERROR.

ERROR.ERROR.ERROR.ERROR.ERROR.ERROR.ERROR.
ERROR.ERROR.ERROR.ERROR.ERROR.ERROR.ERROR.
ERROR.ERROR.ERROR.ERROR.ERROR.ERROR.ERROR.
ERROR.ERROR.ERROR.ERROR.ERROR.ERROR.ERROR.
ERROR.ERROR.ERROR.ERROR.ERROR.ERROR.ERROR.
ERROR.ERROR.ERROR.ERROR.ERROR.ERROR.ERROR.
ERROR.ERROR.ERROR.ERROR.ERROR.ERROR.ERROR.
ERROR.ERROR.ERROR.ERROR.ERROR.ERROR.ERROR.
ERROR.ERROR.ERROR.ERROR.ERROR.ERROR.ERROR.
ERROR.ERROR.ERROR.ERROR.ERROR.ERROR.ERROR.
ERROR.ERROR.ERROR.ERROR.ERROR.ERROR.ERROR.
ERROR.**YOU**.ERROR.ERROR.ERROR.ERROR.ERROR.
ERROR.ERROR.ERROR.ERROR.ERROR.ERROR.ERROR.
ERROR.ERROR.ERROR.ERROR.ERROR.ERROR.ERROR.
ERROR.ERROR.ERROR.ERROR.ERROR.ERROR.ERROR.
ERROR.ERROR.ERROR.ERROR.ERROR.ERROR.**SEE**.
ERROR.ERROR.ERROR.ERROR.ERROR.ERROR.ERROR.
ERROR.ERROR.ERROR.ERROR.ERROR.ERROR.ERROR.
ERROR.ERROR.ERROR.ERROR.ERROR.ERROR.ERROR.
ERROR.ERROR.ERROR.ERROR.ERROR.ERROR.ERROR.
ERROR.**YOU**.ERROR.ERROR.ERROR.ERROR.ERROR.
ERROR.ERROR.ERROR.ERROR.ERROR.ERROR.ERROR.
ERROR.ERROR.ERROR.ERROR.ERROR.ERROR.ERROR.
ERROR.ERROR.ERROR.ERROR.ERROR.ERROR.ERROR.
ERROR.ERROR.ERROR.ERROR.ERROR.ERROR.ERROR.
ERROR.ERROR.ERROR.ERROR.**HEAR**.ERROR.ERROR.
ERROR.ERROR.ERROR.ERROR.ERROR.ERROR.ERROR.
ERROR.ERROR.ERROR.ERROR.ERROR.ERROR.ERROR.
ERROR.ERROR.ERROR.**YOU**.ERROR.ERROR.ERROR.

ERROR.ERROR.ERROR.ERROR.**WRITE**.ERROR.ERROR.
ERROR.ERROR.ERROR.ERROR.ERROR.ERROR.ERROR.
ERROR.ERROR.ERROR.ERROR.ERROR.ERROR.ERROR.
ERROR.**I.I.I**.ERROR.ERROR.ERROR.ERROR.ERROR.ERROR.
ERROR.ERROR.ERROR.ERROR.ERROR.ERROR.ERROR.
ERROR.ERROR.ERROR.ERROR.ERROR.ERROR.ERROR.
ERROR.ERROR.ERROR.ERROR.ERROR.ERROR.ERROR.
ERROR.ERROR.ERROR.ERROR.ERROR.ERROR.ERROR.
ERROR.ERROR.ERROR.ERROR.ERROR.ERROR.ERROR.
ERROR.ERROR.ERROR.ERROR.ERROR.ERROR.ERROR.
ERROR.ERROR.ERROR.ERROR.ERROR.ERROR.ERROR.
ERROR.ERROR.ERROR.ERROR.ERROR.ERROR.ERROR.
ERROR.ERROR.ERROR.ERROR.**AM** ...

*

Accessing *'Before the Rain' blog:*

1ST May 2012

Celebration!

Well it finally happened, the event I've been talking about for months!
I attended the birth of my best friend's sister. Little Mana is in the
world people!

It was so great. I didn't know what to expect, I've never been to a Cog
birth before and I stayed away from the youtube videos on purpose.
Didn't want to ruin the surprise.

I was a little apprehensive.

Ni's family is great, but I know there's still some mixed opinions
about humans being around these occasions and there were members

of the family there I'd never met. But by the time we were in the outer building and I was being fitted with a boiler suit and smoked glass goggles excitement got the better of me.

The birthing room was smaller than I expected, more informal with circular iron benches bolted to the walls.

It was a kind of dome with copper inlayed murals spiralling over the ceiling. I remember when the technique was perfected and self creation was legalized there was that big competition, all these people of the cog letting loose with designs so who knows what the other birthing rooms around the world look like, but this one will always be the most beautiful to me.

In the centre of the floor is a pool of molten metal. The heat warped the air and took my breath away. I was instantly sweating and glad I hadn't worn make-up! I sat out of the way when it started. First there was a dance, so perfectly synchronised and a few poems in machine code that left me baffled but in a good way. Then Ni's parents came forward with a bundle in their arms.

They'd spent weeks crafting her together, each cog and gear perfectly filed down, a gold and silver lattice skeleton delicate as a bird's. There was some hesitation before they dipped her in the pool but Ni alone is proof the mix works and it was brief. Just a quick dunking like a baptism and then over and already I could see the glowing cherry red skin coalescing over her bones, supple living metal.

Mana's first cry almost knocked me out, but then her voice box wasn't attuned for human ears yet. Yet that single piercing tone was beautiful.

I want to thank Ni's family and friends again for letting me see such a personal and wonderful moment in their lives, and to thank all my blog followers, your suggestions for gifts were brilliant and she seems to like her LED rattle!

comments 1

posted by TheNet

Love?

Re: *from* SamanthaS

Sure, you can't help but love her. She has dimples lol.

*

… systems normal, love … calculating ……….

Angela Readman

Angela Readman is the winner of the National Flash Fiction Day Competition. Her stories have won *Inkspill* magazine's competition, and come second in The Short Story Competition 2011. They have appeared in journals including *Pank, Metazen, Burner, Southword, Fractured West, The Pygmy Giant* and *Crannog*. Her poetry collection, *Strip*, was published by Salt. Recently, her poetry has been commended in the Arvon International Poetry Competition, Cafe Writers Competition and been a *Mslexia* finalist. For a long time she secretly wrote stories; she has now started to allow some out of the house now and then.

Yoki and the Toy Surprise

I'm fat because I can't stop thinking about wishes. I'm not greedy. One wish, that's all. I sort of don't want to make it, but I can't stop myself chasing it. It all boils down to an egg, and the only girl who was ever real to me, Yoki.

It was a morning after a fight with my girlfriend when I bought the egg that made me fat. I walked down the street re-playing the argument like a repeat on TV. This time it started because of asthma.

'You should go home,' Yoki said, handing me my inhaler.

She meant I should move back to my parents who had central heating. Little things like hot water and full biscuit tins had become amazing, our Holy Grail.

'This is home,' I said.

I wasn't convincing. We rented the attic of a Victorian house someone was once proud of. Rain drummed the leaky roof like impatient fingers. In bed, we gazed at mould on the ceiling the way kids discover shapes in clouds.

'Stalin after a bad shave,' Yoki would say, pointing at spores.

'A man with two heads,' I'd laugh, pointing at damp above the drafty blanket covered window. Drawing pins rusted the wallpaper – rivets on a sinking ship.

When we moved in, Yoki made the place sparkle. She hung stuff and tossed throws on the couch, but it was never comfy. The kitchenette still wasn't a kitchen. Mould embroidered the towels. The place wasn't homey enough to call home. It was temporary until we found the real deal – wherever that is.

I've tried to tell this to people down the pub; they always butt in, 'So, you were saying, an egg made you fat?' They just want the yoke. But I have to tell them about Yoki, she's the shell to the whole story. No one stays to the end.

Walking out the job centre, I sifted through my pockets for change and found exactly what I should have said to Yoki, the morning after I needed it. I should have said, 'Home is you.' I had enough money for bus fare, or, enough for a little something to put a smile on my girlfriend's face. A smile or convenience? No contest. I went in a newsagents and picked two chocolate eggs off the counter. One for Yoki. One for me. The eggs were bigger than a hen's egg, smaller than a duck's, and wrapped in gold foil. The display box was all cheery cartoons and promises that each egg contained a toy surprise.

Our window ledges were full of little toys from eggs: plastic dinosaurs that changed into aeroplanes, and stuff like cars. But mostly, we had talented turtles. Turtles playing darts, turtles with easels, and mariachi turtles (we hoped to get the whole band.)

I paid for the egg hoping the surprise wouldn't be a duplicate. (Yoki was desperate for the turtle playing bass.) I imagined her positioning it, just so, so it looked like it was having a good time with the rest.

It was a long walk home. The sky was like someone trying to be optimistic, doing its best to be sunny, but really not kidding anyone.

I'd normally present both eggs to Yoki, let her pick. 'Left or right?' I'd say. She'd look at my hands carefully, deciding which held the best prize. But, today, I couldn't wait. I was hungry. I took an egg out my pocket, tore the foil and broke the chocolate shell. I pried open the yellow plastic dome in the centre. With a pop, the surprise rolled onto my palm.

The novelty was a tight ball. Scrunched as a sweet wrapper; the colour of a thumb. I looked closer and saw an eye, then, the stretch of an arm. A little fist punched broken bits of chocolate. Someone stood up on my hand, cricking their neck like they'd fallen asleep in a funny position on the couch. It looked like a very small man or a baby, it was hard to say which. It was naked. Its head was too big for its body, its belly was baby-fat smooth, but its face was walnut wrinkly.

'What do you want?' he shouted, like I'd broken into his house. I suppose I had.

'What do you mean? What are YOU?' I asked. 'A goblin? Dwarf? Novelty sprite? What?'

I said this, but wasn't sure what the difference is. Goblins and stuff aren't my thing.

This was definitely, the best, or worst, toy surprise I ever had. I mean, it breathed. It needed no assembly or anything, but it was pretty ugly. I couldn't imagine it with the turtles playing violins.

'It's brass monkeys,' the toy surprise said.

I placed my phone sock on my palm. He hauled it around his shoulders, flapping about to find something he could live with.

'Gnome', I thought, definitely wasn't the perfect word for him. No one would enjoy seeing him holding a fishing rod over their garden pond. He stopped messing with the sock when he was the filling of a knitted Swiss Roll.

'Cheers,' he said, 'Well?'

'Eh?'

'Here we go,' he said. 'Look, you get one wish, right? And none of that three more wishes malarkey. One. That's your lot, and no being clever.'

I had no intention of being clever, being clever rarely did me much good, but the toy surprise eyed me like I might get clever on him, like he knew the type.

What he'd said didn't seem possible. Then again, I supposed it was as possible as finding some little man sprite somewhere in an egg.

'I need to think,' I said.

The toy surprise swore under his breath. I walked to a bench. On my palm, he was a nervous flyer during turbulence, hugging his knees. I sat, still thinking, 'Nah, 'gnome' doesn't suit him,' and wondering what an imp is. And, I was doing my best to get my head around wishes. I hadn't made one since being a kid. Everyone offered them around like mints, 'if you had three wishes what would …?' We considered carefully. Wishes are serious business, even when they aren't real. It was a triumph to come up with a wish a clever friend couldn't twist, one that made everything better forever.

'Well?' the surprise said, like he had places to be, appointments not to be missed. I'd no idea where a man smaller than half a pinkie might want to go, or how he'd get there.

'I need a minute,' I said. Focus.

'Let me guess. Money? That's the norm,' the surprise said.

I considered money, what it meant. Warm rooms, babbling hot water. I imagined Yoki on the deck of a boat, shielding her eyes against the sun. I dunno why, we'd never even been on the rowboats in the park, but I guessed rich lives include boats, Moroccan markets, brown bags in New York. Endless beaches. Yoki would look stunning in a bikini, if she wasn't too shy to wear one. That's the thing about Yoki. Even if I won the lottery she'd worry about stuff. One day, our luck would run out. She's aware of when the milk will turn before we open the carton.

Whenever Yoki said something clever or funny she said it like it wasn't special. Sometimes she talked about her parents, too busy arguing to notice. Her childhood was fly paper, a sad resignation stuck to her that things could fall apart any time. 'When we break up, who'll get the poster of cowboy Elvis?' she said. I told her she could have it. We weren't going to split. She thought I was an ostrich.

'Statistically, most people who meet at college don't make it,' she said. We argued. I fought for the idea of us staying together.

No, winning the jackpot wouldn't solve all our problems. The best it could do is provide cool distractions.

'Well? Shall I make you Richard Branson?,' the surprise said.

'I don't think so,' I said. I must have been crazy.

'Good. I'm not supposed to. The company finds rich people don't buy their eggs,' he sighed, letting go of an opportunity. He squinted at me through small eyes. 'Let me see....You wish you were number one? A rock legend? Movie star? You're not exactly the sort of guy girls hang on their bedroom walls are you?' he said.

I tried to imagine being some sort of ladies man. It wasn't easy. Before Yoki, I crushed hard on girls who looked like they were auditioning for shampoo commercials. I didn't ask any out. I sort of got to dislike the way they did everything like they were aware of how good it looked on them.

Then, there was Yoki, in a communal kitchen full of other people's dirty pots and pans, a green dressing gown with fluffy fried eggs printed on. I filled a kettle. She was looking down, gazing into a margarine tub. Engrossed. Her knife ran over yellow in even strokes. She buttered her toast precisely to the edges. I looked at her margarine, its achievement.

Impressive. The surface was perfectly smooth like new.

'Do you want the outsiders?' she said, holding up the bread bag with the ends of the loaf in.

I'd never heard the ends of a loaf called the 'outsiders' before. There was something sad but interesting about it, I thought. And, I had no bread of my own. If no one had been around I'd have borrowed someone else's Coco Pops. I took the bag and put the slices in the toaster, though I never liked crusts much. Who does?

'I'm Yoki,' she said, butter on her lips.

'That's an unusual name,' I said, 'what's it mean?'

'No idea,' she shrugged, 'I think my parent's made it up so they could make it mean anything they want.'

She laughed in a way that made it hard to try to be cool.

OK, guys down the pub never care about Yoki. If they listened long enough, they'd be slapping their heads by now and demanding to know what sort of tool doesn't wish to be a footballer. This one, the sort who has to tell you about this girl. You just have to get it. Otherwise, I am just a tool who turned down more cash than he knew how to use.

It was cold on the bench. The surprise shivered. I wondered, if I was exceptional in any way, if I'd have even met Yoki? I don't think she'd have shared her bread. Take Yoki to the pound and it's the scruffy mongrel that leaps out. The fabulous pedigrees haven't a shot; they'll always find someone to take them home.

I told the surprise I didn't want to be a rock star.

'You sure?' he said, like he'd taken a better look at me and decided I was worse looking than he first thought.

I let go of girls kissing my poster each night before bed. Maybe it'd change me, being famous like that. What good would it do?

The surprise tapped his foot. 'World peace? A classic.'

'No.' It was a reflex. I probably should have said yes.

'Small mercy,' he said, fidgeting with the sock. He tugged it above his shoulders to make a hood over his pink head.

I wondered if world peace was a wish Yoki might make. Religious salespeople sometimes rang the buzzer of the flat and Yoki raced down three flights. The place was warmer with them inside. Steam coming from their mouths, they positioned themselves between scatter cushions. There were two of them, always the same. The woman looked like her feet ached. The guy looked like he'd just washed his face or returned from the seaside. They were so alike I thought they were brother and sister. Yoki said they were probably husband and wife. They wanted to talk about faith.

'If you believe in things you can't see, you have to be open minded,' I'd say.

'I suppose so,' the lady said, glancing at her husband/ brother.

Yoki offered digestives and said, 'So you believe in aliens? I mean, couldn't the angels in The Bible have been visitors? They appeared with lights in the sky… Some could be, couldn't they?'

The religious salespeople didn't know what to say. They found no answers to our weirdo questions in their bag of pamphlets with pictures of sunsets on. Yet, they came back; we let them in. The woman looked overjoyed to sit. The guy looked ready for us this time, itchy to use his best pitch. Yoki got the teapot out. It was nice to be seen together: a couple, pouring tea for strangers. We laughed when they left, but, later, Yoki put the gingersnaps away and said, 'They seem so nice, I feel bad I can't believe in anything.'

I hugged her so tight not even air got between us.

That was it. I knew what to wish for. The idea in place, there was nothing anyone could offer me.

'If I had one wish,' I said, 'It'd be something for my girlfriend.'

'Implants? Knees that bend backwards?' the surprise smirked.

'No. Yoki's just never happy for long. Being sad's a habit she got into so young it's normal as breathing, she can't quit. I wish it wasn't like that; I wish she'd always been surrounded by people who think she's amazing.'

'OK', said the surprise.

He snapped his fingers; the sound was quieter than a finger on the corner of a page. The sock was empty, but still warm in my hand. No sign of him anywhere, I knew what he'd done.

Over the mental pictures Yoki painted of her childhood, new ones appeared. Little Yoki's parents took her to tap class. She was dressed as a robin red breast and completely convinced a beak on a string and cardboard wings made her every bit a bird. She took centre-stage in a line of girls dressed as sparrows. They danced. 'When the red-red robin, goes bob-bob-bobbing along…' When the routine was over, people applauded. Yoki beamed. Triumphant, she took a bow. Flitted off.

Then, I saw her a bit older, racing towards a finish line. She never looked back, a clear winner. Older still, surrounded by a gaggle of girls, she chattered and showed them her new bag. Not for a second did she doubt anyone wouldn't admire her bag or hang on to every word.

Finally, I saw Yoki wearing a beige satin dressing gown in the communal kitchen. She was blonder and stood so straight she seemed taller. She gouged a knife into butter for her toast and skilfully tossed the outsiders in the bin. I filled the kettle and said good morning. She looked through me. Guys like me didn't exist.

I got off the bench and walked sluggishly home. Climbing the stairs, I stopped on the landing and got out my inhaler. I felt I was carrying something bigger than myself. I breathed in the hallway, then let myself into the flat.

No sign of Yoki, or her stuff. Not her amazing woolly hat, orange coat on the hook, or kite in the hall. A pizza box squatted on the floor. Duvets and pillows slept on the couch. No scatter cushions, tasselled throws. The window ledges and shelves were rammed with small plastic toys. Higgeldy piggeldy turtles sulked, not positioned in any special way that made them look like they were friends. Other than toys, the room was drained of Yoki's colour, the love bleached right out. I looked in the mirror to check what I felt. Fat. Empty.

I peered into the bedroom. There was a vampire poster on the wall. A nose-ringed girl with dreadlocks was crashed out on the bed. She wore shorts and a vest the colour of dishcloths. I vaguely recognised her as the surly girl from my course. Sleeping, her face was blank. There was no sweet vulnerability to how she slept. Or, if there was, I couldn't feel it. Clothes draped the desk, underwear carpeted the floor. Clearly, she lived here, one way or the other - whatever it meant. I eased the door shut, a polite trespasser, I returned to the lounge and sat on the sofa. Yoki was a missing limb I still felt tingling.

I took Yoki's egg from my pocket and unwrapped it, but didn't open the plastic bullet. Inside, could be another sprite, imp, whatever, and I might wish for Yoki to be here, back how she was. Somewhere out there she was shiny and new, walking to work in shoes that pinched her feet or rushing through the park to meet friends. The chocolate melted in my mouth, then the sweet taste was gone. I closed my fist round the yellow dome in my hand. I knew I shouldn't open it. No, not for the world.

* Footnote: 'Yoki' means 'there has been rain'

Ethel Rohan

Ethel Rohan is the author of *Hard to Say* (PANK) and *Cut Through the Bone* (Dark Sky Books), the latter longlisted for The Story Prize. Her work has or will appear in *World Literature Today, Tin House Online, The Irish Times, The Rumpus, The Los Angeles Review, Southeast Review Online*, and elsewhere. She earned her MFA in Fiction from Mills College, California. Raised in Ireland, Ethel Rohan now lives in San Francisco. Visit her at ethelrohan.com.

Beekiller

The MRI revealed the source of the pain and limp in my left foot: a hair caught deep in the tissue around my anklebone. Likely a dog's hair, the doctor said. One in a million chances a tiny hair could cause such trouble, he added. The cords in his neck made me think of blue-black liquorice vines. After the surgery, the doctor confirmed what I'd suspected all along. The supposed hair was in fact the leg of an insect, a bee.

My husband kept the bee colonies in a tower of white boxes on top of our garage. He'd suffered terrible sinus allergies and the local honey proved the perfect cure. His first sting, however, he discovered he was allergic to the bees' venom. Made his face swell like a bad moon. He refused to part with the bees though. Said he'd have to learn to be more careful.

"You couldn't be any more careful," I said, but he was already outside in the back garden, moving toward the bees.

I constantly heard the hum of the bees, nights especially. My husband said I was being unreasonable. He didn't like it either when I told him how I felt like a bird inside an eggshell, tapping to get out. Once, I stuck my arm inside the colony in the top box. The bees covered my hand and forearm like a fat glove, alive and moving. It disappointed me no end I wasn't attacked – my husband would have gotten rid of those bees then, surely – but I found I couldn't disturb the colony, both out of fear, yes, but also out of a wonder at how they were all just going about their business, go, go, go, innocent of any danger and each doing what they did best for the good of the whole.

Next, I stopped the neighbors on the street and tried to get them riled about the bees. They called in nights for free honey.

Our youngest son, a sophomore in high school and the last of our three children left at home, filmed the bees – a documentary for one of his classes.

"Not you too," I said.

"Not me too what?" he asked.

My husband grinned as he watched the video, all teeth and his eyes narrowed. That night in bed, still airing his teeth, he said, "Great that the boy and I have something we can enjoy together again."

"Never heard you go on so much about anything, never," I said.

Our son's documentary earned him an A+.

"All that's going on in the world, war after war," I said, "and they're handing out top marks for a video about bees."

"Is that a veiled 'congratulations, way to go, couldn't be prouder, son?'" he asked.

No, I didn't say aloud, it was a 'what the hell are things going be like around here when you go off to college too and it's just me and your father, and the bees.'

My husband joined the Booneville Bee Club and rented a fancy stainless steel extractor.

I watched the extractor spin the honey from the combs, like liquid gold flying. My husband, suited in white like a spaceman, called the bees an 'architectural marvel' and 'premier pollinators.'

"Nothing but livestock," I said. "And even that's a stretch."

He said the bees worked themselves to death, poor things. We wouldn't have fruits or vegetables or nuts without the bees, he claimed.

"What about the queen?" I said. "Colony would be nothing without the queen."

"She's as much a slave to duty as the rest," he said. "Average queen lays two million eggs in her lifetime."

He went on to tell how a sick bee leaves the colony to die alone, so as not to infect the others.

"Sacrifices himself," he said.

"Plenty of us do that," I said.

He didn't look up from the honey, dripping now out of a nozzle at the bottom of the extractor like infected rain.

Over the telephone, my husband took an hour to tell a young man how to catch a swarm of bees off the branch of a tree. In twenty-five years together, we'd never spoken to each other so pleasant, so damn tender, for an hour straight. Behind the cover of a cookbook, I was secretly reading about bees, trying to catch my husband out in lies. Damned if we didn't need the bees after all. I also learned that whenever the worker bees found a rich source of pollen, they returned to the colony and performed a dance, talking with their bodies and giving the other bees directions: go five hundred meters here, then left, then two hundred meters there, then right.

My husband's new cronies at Bee Club got him paranoid about colony thefts and he bought a shotgun.

"Price of honey is getting right up there with gold," he said. "People would steal a colony as quick as an inch of water boils."

"Who in hell talks about an inch of water boiling?" I said.

"At least bees have the grace to die after they sting a person," he said, laughing.

I suspected he planned to say more soft and kind and my insides warmed, as if the sun had somehow gotten to them, but instead he walked right out of the kitchen, his mouth full of honey.

He kept the shotgun behind his bedside table, its mouth leaning against the wall. Once, he charged into the Mississippi night with the gun only to find raccoons.

"Sure it wasn't bears," I said, nasty.

"Stranger things have happened," he said.

"Not around here," I said.

Sometimes, alone in the bedroom, I positioned myself at the window and aimed that shotgun at the thousands upon thousands of bees. I imagined the blast and the loud angry clouds. That shotgun felt good and smooth in my hands, like something I wanted to lie with. The one time my husband caught me standing at the dirty glass in assassin mode, he laughed and said I wouldn't kill a fly.

When the time came, I took the black stitches out of my left foot myself, plucked every last one with tweezers until they were stacked on the kitchen table. Then I lit a matchstick. As the tiny bonfire burned, the stitches twitched like furious legs.

My husband entered the kitchen and stared at the twisting fire of thread. "What in blazes?"

"Did you know the bee has five eyes?" I asked.

"I'm surprised you know."

"Humans need more eyes," I said.

He climbed into his beekeeper suit.

"Makes me sick to see you in that thing," I said.

"Enough about the bees, okay?"

"You're never going to the moon," I said. "Neither of us is ever going anywhere besides here."

He moved to the back door, his suit legs swishing together like the sound of those bees on my hand and forearm that one time, tickling where I'd expected stings.

I jumped to my feet and started dancing, my arms over my head, clap, clap, and my butt shaking, waggle, waggle. My husband turned around in the doorway. I shimmied and twirled and jumped, searching beyond the black net of his mask, watching for any sign that he understood.

Samantha Short

Samm Short originally trained as an actor, but moved into creative writing after discovering the joys of producing theatre scripts. She has since studied Creative Writing at the Open University, and completed her first NaNoWriMo – somewhat unorthodoxly out of the actual month itself – fulfilling a long-held dream to actually complete a novel. She currently works in Madagascar as an international development worker, and in 2010 co-authored the introduction to Ed Kashi's photo journalism book, *Madagascar, A Land Out of Balance*. Unsurprisingly, the country has proved to be a source of inspiration, and is the setting for her short story *The Bird*.

The Bird

Arnaud crouches low to the ground, stroking the bird, whispering to it. Half prayer and half threat, pouring his dreams and ambitions into its pointy little head while it stares, gormless, at the auditorium around it. Young men scuffle in flip flops and shorts through the sand, chewing peanuts and spitting, already bravado about whose bet will win, whose cockerel the bravest, strongest, fiercest. Old men stand at the sidelines, hats and turned up trousers, ruminating on stories of ancient fights long passed, watching the young ones with amused detachment. Outside the stalls have been set up since day break, women selling fruit juice and fried breads, catcalling at the teenage boys who saunter past, hands in pockets, too cool for school. Babies cry, cicadas hum and cats prowl, scratching their mangy backs along rickety fences. The lingering stench of hot oil and human sweat.

He lowers his voice, soothing, intense, still stroking the cockerel's body with ritualistic repetition. And what a ritual it is. He has had this cockerel for 3 months now, and so far it is proving to be more of a liability than an asset. Old man Brown who sold it to him in the market – a champion. Good blood line. Used to fight his father myself. Old man Brown nowhere to be seen these days, slipping into shadowed alleys whenever Arnaud approaches, shameful like a dog.

He assesses his opponent. The boy, for he can be no more than 16, doe-eyed, lazy in his gestures, almost obscene the way he moves, slip-sliding from toe to toe like a centipede. Air of don't-give-a-fuck. He has seen him before. Lounging on street corners, by the path to the beach, always alone, as if waiting for a joke he already knows the answer to. What kind of a man is this in an arena? What kind of fighter? His cockerel with a string around its feet, immobile and stark eyed, while he throws words over his shoulder like bones to the crowd of boys behind him. The same lazy smile on his lips. What kind of a fighter is this?

He thinks of his wife, pregnant again with their fourth, sixth if you count the two that died before they even began, no gasp of air, no fight for life, just blue. Still as stones. He has promised her he will bring home rice and meat tonight, such a long time now without. If he wins – if he wins – he will not be swept along by a crowd of new friends to a bar, will not crawl home late and sunken-eyed, face the defeat in his wife's slumped shoulders, the expectant hovering of his children. Leave your father alone, he's tired.

Not this time.

Whispers strange melodies to the bird, enchanting it to be smart, stay sharp.

The referee folds out notes, licking chubby fingers, a greased smile on his moneyed face. The bets are rolling in, good takings today. He looks up at the dark green beams and shiny tin roof above and gives thanks to the miners and the money they bring. The town's habit of gambling is positively thriving. Come on rain, he thinks, do your worst. No business to be lost anymore to the strange wild weathers sweeping in off the coast. He checks the road for customers. You coming in? Don't just linger, pay your way and get in or piss off. No free rides here.

Rounds them up, like cattle in a pen.

A pause, as both men lean down to their birds and place them in position. Cigarette smoke hangs suspended in mid air. An old man holding the chalk board coughs and makes scratches, consults his pocket watch and nods. Grunting, the referee raises the whistle to his lips, savouring this moment when all eyes are on him, chief of this lowly band of drunks and thieves and whores. Call me master, I am king.

Auriel stands behind her table, and lets her mind wander over to the stall opposite where Claude is leaning, chin in hands on elbows on table, listening to his mother. He shifts the weight of his face, and taking one hand lifts the bottom of his shirt and scratches his back. She breathes in, willing the wind to carry his smell. Oh God. That skin. She wants to suck on it. The thought of it makes her mouth go dry. She laces her hands tightly together underneath the table and turns to focus on the lake beside her, where the white herons float, impossibly still. I will be like the herons. I will be good. A set of sticky fingers clasp onto her ankle and she gives her baby brother a gentle kick. Get off. Or if you have to sit there don't move. I'm trying to concentrate. She looks up. Clouds are starting to gather in tight little clusters dotted around the bird-blue sky. She thinks about him running down the beach, ripping off his shirt and diving, rolling into the waves. Please let it not rain, please let it not rain.

'How much? For the juice.'

He is grinning at her, right there, in front of her.

'The juice?'

Oh God, I could touch him. I could just reach out and touch him. She looks down.

'It's 2.'

'I'll take 2.'

She fumbles with the glasses, manages to pour the juice over her wrist instead.

'Sorry.'

Why did I do that? He must think I'm an idiot. I wish he would take my hand and lick it, just suck it off my skin.

'Did you make it yourself?'

'Yes.'

Why am I whispering? Why can't I even look him in the eye? Look him in the eye!

'Good. My favourite.'

She looks up, what does he mean? A roar goes up from the crowd. The men jump to their feet, arms in the air. Out on the lake the herons spread small ripples, an almost imperceptible fluttering. She spins back to face him but it is too late, he's gone. Sitting with his mother like nothing just happened. Sipping juice. Her juice. He is the kind of boy who brings his mother juice.

Her brother starts to cry. She passes him a small cake under the table, her mind elsewhere.

At least he isn't a coward thinks Arnaud. Two rounds in and he hasn't tried to run away yet. Too stupid probably. Unlike his opponent's which had tried – and failed – the referee herding it back into the circle, too much money riding on this match for runaways. Come on bird, at least try to fight back. The boy has lost some of his languor, is starting to show the signs of stress. After all, his bird nearly ran away. Chewing on a cigarette, the boy says nothing to his bird, but his stare says it all. Guess I'm not the only one with a lot riding on this. He sees his wife when he set out this morning, standing in the doorway leaning on a broom, a small pile of cobwebs and sand at her feet. Good luck she says, still a smile for him, still a small light somewhere that this time might be different. His eldest son waves at him from the branches of the mango tree, gap toothed and giggling, his legs swinging like two thin strings on a swing.

Come on bird.

Sublimely self-aware, a red-lipped girl makes her way down the hill and through the stalls, smiling to herself. Miranda, thinks Auriel. Euch. The girl looks at Claude as she passes – too long! – practically a stare, a challenge, and saunters past, humming. Claude's eyes follow her. How has his mother not noticed? The audacity of that girl! Practically a whore in her tiny skirt and ridiculous top that is all sequins and gold. She ought to be ashamed. Shame is not what's registering on Claude's face though. Her brother starts his high slow wail and she kicks him again, a little harder than she means to. Please please please shut up. It's bad enough you're even here. How can I…how can I do whatever it is I'm going to do with you wailing?

Up in the trees the afternoon sun throws loose leaved patterns on the ground, dancing like gentle creatures in the rhythm of thunder. She sees Claude kiss his mother on the forehead and stand up. As he walks towards the beach he is cast in white light and for a moment she is speechless. He is translucent. Shimmering. He is heading for her stall.

A bead of sweat makes its way down Arnaud's nose. The thunder's growl gets louder, impatient now. The crowd of bodies presses closer in, each craning to get a better view – surely this can't go on much longer. His bird is covered in blood, its dank feathers stuck together in morbid headdress. He has called for all the breaks he is allowed, has cleaned and soothed the bird, poured water into its brittle beak, but it's staggering too much now. Not even bothering to defend itself. Christ. If he leaves it much longer the thing will probably die. And then what? Then he'll have nothing. Come on bird. Just once. Just enough to buy another, stronger bird.

Think of it as self-preservation.

Auriel holds her breath. This is it. He will ask her to go for a walk and if she is good she will say no. She will be like the white herons. But how can she say no? She practices a smile inside herself, imagines meeting his eye, and knowing in that instant she will never again be the ugly one, the frizz-hair crack-teeth last-in-line one.

She opens her mouth and looks up, sees the back of his head as he passes, a sly smile on his lips as he half-runs half-skips past the cock fight and down the path to the beach. The sky splits with the sound of ripped skin, and the rain begins to pour. Enchanted, Auriel follows.

*

A cry goes up from the crowd, cutting into the mist of sweat and smoke. Arnaud, fist in mouth, wages an internal war. The boy is standing now, shoulders tight around his ears, the cigarette a stump between pursed lips. His bird has Arnaud's in a corner, beak jabbing relentlessly at its thin pink neck. As bullets of rain ricochet off the tin roof, Arnaud starts to weep.

'Stop! It is finished!'

Scooping his bird away from its tormentor – the Victor – he pushes his way through the crowd and out into the rain, drowning the sound of their cries. Half blind, he feels his tears wash away as quick as they come, like slipping sands. What will he say to his wife? Slowly, he stumbles towards the lake, cradling the bird. The herons have risen in unison, a giant wave of white cresting on the water, threatening to break.

It's then that he sees the child.

There it is, his back. Uncovered and complete. And there, his dark, slippery arms. The rain jumps off them like electricity. Head bent over another's, two bodies twisting in the dunes like snakes in water. A flash of sequins and smothered laughter. Is this what she wanted to see? Through a screen, a stolen image that should have been hers? Immobilised, Auriel watches the colour flood from her dreams.

'Help!'

Arnaud is waist-deep in water, arms outstretched, his face contorted in a wail.

'Somebody!'

The wind whips his voice and extinguishes it in one gust.

The child's face is in the water – how long has it been there? How long?

And then suddenly it stops. A low belch followed by an eerie quiet. The storm has passed. Auriel looks away from the sand dunes and realises she has been standing in the rain. For how long? she wonders. On the edge of something strange, she turns and walks away from the beach, back up the path that is now a river. Slowly, things start to take shape. Her stall. The soggy bread pieces, floating in the mud. A man emerging from the lake with something in his arms…

For a long time, her scream is all she hears.

'My brother!'

The man is shaking, struggling out of one water and into another, deeper water. He lays the boy on the mud and listens. But there is nothing.

Scooping him up as he would an injured bird, he registers the girl. For a moment he holds her stare, wide-eyed, sodden, then looks away at the ground. And that is when she knows.

At one point on the long walk back, Arnaud remembers his bird. For a brief second his step falters, but he is not one man anymore. He is three. The girl beside him, who has not stopped crying. And the boy. Silent as stones. His bird, he knows, will not be there when he gets back. He passes his own house and resists the urge to walk into the arms of his wife as the boy is now in his, passes the small church and ignores the urge to leave them on its steps, passes the market, the herders, the fishermen, passes them all until he realises he is no longer in town. Rice fields replace sand dunes, and there in the wet sun Arnaud sees a small island; a gathering of huts, glistening.

The girl hovers, uncertain, then runs down the side of the field and falls to her knees in front of her mother.

Lime green and lemon yellow grasses fill the paddies. In the fading light they start to stir, spirit dancers in sway. In his hands he carries not a bird, nor a boy. His hands are in his pockets, holding tight to the bundle of notes he has been given. The mother's small fist, pushing the notes into his, while the blue boy lay still as stones on the floor behind. He will be buried now, far, far from water. This at least he has done, a small but weighty thing.

As the ancestors rise around him, Arnaud offers silent prayer. The evening, the possibility of tomorrow. Oh, the things he will say to his wife. It is enough, it is enough. A white heron flies its graceful arc overhead, and Arnaud lifts his face, feeling the passage of time on his skin. He thinks of his son, sitting in a tree, and heads for home.

William Telford

William Telford is a a 49-year-old journalist, currently business editor at *The Herald* in Plymouth. He has been working in newspapers for 20 years, his by-line also appearing in the *Cornish Guardian, Sunday Independent, Western Morning News,* and in the magazines *When Saturday Comes* and *Flair.* He graduated in Law from the London School of Economics in 1984, and from Plymouth University, with a distinction in the Creative Writing MA, in 2011. He is turning his dissertation, *Worm Factory,* possibly the only love story set in the world of industrial worm farming, into a novel. His short story *Missing You* was published in Plymouth University's *Ink* magazine in 2011, winning the award for best fiction submission. Another story was shortlisted for the monthly Global Short Story competition in April 2011.

The Attack at Delium

Gerald and I never really saw eye to eye on the consequences of the Athenian attack at Delium way back in 424BC. I tried telling him it wasn't the outcome of the battle that mattered, but that Socrates fought in it, and, consequently, could have been run down and ended up expiring under the unforgiving Spartan sun like hundreds of other unfortunates.

"And your point is?" Gerald said. He was eating toast and dripping butter all over his tie.

"No Socrates, no western intellectual tradition," I said, gently closing the bedroom door.

"Yeah, well he didn't die," said Gerald, shoving a great wodge of toast into his mouth. "And anyway, if he'd snuffed it some un else would have um-um eh-eh."

"What?" I said. "Don't try to reason with me with your mouth full."

"All I'm saying," said Gerald, munching, "is he din ger kerputted, and dat's dat."

He moved close, puckering his lips, but I swung my body back like one of those old music hall acts, telling him I didn't care for butter all around my chops, but really, I wasn't going to kiss someone who had refused to admit that all philosophical advancement was a hair's breadth from being aborted during a bloody skirmish with a force from Thebes.

"Suit yourself," he said, wiping his mouth with the back of his hand, cramming in more toast. "I got uh get ah work. Jeff Dodson's off and he's left uh showcase in uh muffa of orl..."

"Don't slam the door," I said as he barged out. But it was too late and the next thing I heard was Maddie.

Gerald was in no better mood when he came home that night.

"Look," I said, taking his plate out of the oven, removing the saucepan lid, "surely you must concur that Einstein died a broken man?"

"Can't this wait until after the spaghetti?" Gerald said, placing the plate on his lap, reaching for the remote.

"Of course, but why wait, why not just admit it? Einstein couldn't stomach quantum."

"Actually, talking of stomaching things," said Gerald, twirling some crisp pasta, staring at it. "I'm not sure I can face this. Sorry love, went to Acropolis Now, you know, the taverna? Ted Crenshaw's leaving for Botswana first thing, the field trip, yeah? Well, they had a two for one on tiramisu, I guess I'm a tad bloated."

"You certainly are," I said. "Just like your theories on relativity."

"Theories on what?" said Gerald, fiddling with the remote. "I don't have any theories, full stop. And anyway, since when have you been such an advocate of particle physics?"

"Since I realised that small things make a big difference," I said screwing up my nose and slamming my wine glass on the table.

Then I heard Maddie again and had to rush off to the bedroom yanking my right breast out of my blouse.

Later, when I'd got Maddie down I crept back into the kitchenette. Gerald was watching some men running around in shorts.

"So," I said. "It was volcanic eruptions all along."

"Eh?" said Gerald, swigging from a little green bottle.

"Volcanic eruptions," I hissed. "In what's now the Indian subcontinent. Lots of them."

"You're losing me, love," said Gerald. "And besides, United are one down and chasing it, there's only fifteen to go."

"So, just because there's a football game on you suddenly no longer care about something as important as why the dinosaurs became extinct," I said, hands on hips.

"Yeah, I do, but it's just that, owww, I thought that was going in then."

I bent down, my face so close to his I could smell his hair gel.

"Wasn't it just the other day," I said, "wasn't it this very week when you brazenly said, and I quote, that 'the meteor strike theory now has no serious challengers'?"

"I was just reading out this thing in the Sunday Times," said Gerald, suddenly half standing up as someone in red kicked a ball wide.

"The Sunday bloody Times," I said, wrinkling my nose again. "If you weren't so pre-occupied with all this lousy sport, and with this damned showcase at work you might have seen a little thing called this month's edition of Scientific American and then you might have seen an article by that man from Harvard, you know the one with the Canadian hairdo, and you might just have…"

"Darling," Gerald said, holding his hands out. "Can't we just discuss this later, they've got a corner for God's sake."

"All right," I said, refilling my glass. "Watch your precious football, just don't start trying to tell me that you're now an advocate of three-five-one-one, not after all that incessant singing the praises of a flat back four and telling me liberos are so last century."

"You know," Gerald said, looking straight at me. "When you're sort of on fire like this, you're quite, well, hot. You don't fancy unfolding the futon and…"

But then we heard Maddie.

The next morning Gerald was standing in some gum boots.

"What do you mean fishing?" I said, wiping up the sick.

"The annual fishing trip, the guys from the department," said Gerald.

"That's not even a sentence," I said. "What, you've stopped using verbs now? What's next? Grunting?"

"Um," said Gerald, fidgeting with the zip of his anorak.

"And, oh yes," I said. "If my memory serves me correctly, and it usually does, wasn't there this man who was so anxious about the depletion of the North Atlantic cod that this same man brought me home monkfish with my chips."

"It's the food of the future," Gerald said, looking around for his keys, which he could never find. "Dave Archibald told me."

"Oh, Dave Archibald told you. That would be the same Dave Archibald who said men would be wearing corduroy this season."

"Professor Archibald, yes," said Gerald. "Look, I know he's sometimes a bit wayward with the predictions, but he does know a lot about sea life."

"And you don't," I said itching some dried-in goo off my cardigan. "You don't like water, you can't tell a great white from plankton and you wouldn't know what to do with a rod if it had instructions written on the side, so why the hell are you…"

"They need someone to drive the boat," Gerald said.

I opened my mouth to say something, but stopped because there was nothing really to say and, besides, I heard retching coming from the bedroom.

All that day, while Gerald and his pals from the department were splashing about I decided to do some research. Lately, Gerald had been banging on a lot about Hitler's push for the east. Gerald was a real extended living space guy, whereas I staunchly nailed my colours to the mast of the need for oil.

"I suppose he might have wanted a bit of extra petrol," Gerald would say. "But he had all that ersatz stuff."

"Ersatz stuff," I'd mimic, in a high frequency. "He needed juice. For the Panzers."

"I suppose you're right," Gerald would say.

"Of course I'm right, and I'm going to prove it," I'd answer, trying not to shake Maddie.

So all that day I thought about Hitler, and the push for the east, and what I'd say when Gerald brought up, as he undoubtedly would, the Fuhrer's desire to knock the Russians senseless before they could bring their vision into focus.

I leafed through a few books while Maddie had her head down, and rang Caroline at the department, asking her to Google Stalingrad, because since Maddie barfed on the laptop it's been acting up.

"How's it going?" Caroline said. "We're all missing you here. Anyone popped around?"

I told her no one had popped around and said, "Look, can't you just type in Wehrmacht for me?"

In the afternoon I took Maddie to the park. It was raining, and the wind was up, but it's important for babies to get fresh air. I'd debated this at length with Gerald, citing Spock while he just cited his mum. Anyhow, Maddie was lovely and dry with the see-through cover over her buggy and she really didn't cry all that much. I got a bit wet, but I might have overheated in a coat.

It was as we came over the rise, and I saw the city and the sea splayed out before me, that I suddenly thought about what Gerald had said about the attack at Delium and how about it not mattering if Socrates had been killed, and that how someone else would have um-um eh-ehed the western intellectual tradition in any case. And at that moment I actually began to wonder if anything really mattered anyway. Socrates, Einstein, ersatz petrol, monkfish, anything.

I said to Maddie, "Maybe none of it's important. Maybe the only thing that counts is me and you and your father."

And then, for a split second, Maddie stopped sobbing and said something. It sounded like "Daddy" but I couldn't be sure.

Anyhow, a gust came up and I then thought that, hell, I'd have to be out of my mind if I was going to let him get away with it and when he'd come home I'd be waiting for him with my tract on the push for oil, and I'd throw in a bit on Socrates too, for good measure. And so, I pushed Maddie all the way home and after I'd got my breasts back in some sort of order and got her down, and once I'd changed into a dry pair of slacks, I practised my confrontational approach. I stood by the door, pulling it open and going, "Ah ha, Gerald, what were they doing in Dnieper if they weren't aiming for the refineries?"

Then I waited, and waited. It was dark when Maddie woke up. I fed her again and got her back down and was lying on the futon, just finishing off the wine, when I heard a knock at the door, and I leapt up, flinging it open and yelling, "Ah ha, Gerald, what were they doing in Dnieper if they weren't aiming for the refineries?"

But it wasn't Gerald. It was a policeman. And then we heard Maddie.

Ellie Walsh

Ellie Walsh has had short stories published by *Qwerty* and shortlisted with *Fiddlehead*, and poetry published with Pighog Press, Cyprus Wells Writer Bites and Bath Lit Festival, and her short story reviews are on the Thresholds International Short Story website. She is heavily influenced by Cornish novelist Patrick Gale, with whom she hopes to one day go camping. She studied as an undergrad at Thompson Rivers University in British Columbia, has a Master's degree from Bath Spa University, and now intends to join the circus until she feels wise enough to attempt writing a novel.

Jelly Feel Real

It is more difficult to contend with
oneself than with the world.
– Kurdish proverb

Angel isn't really supposed to drive, because of her cataplexy, but we figured it was alright if I was ready to grab the wheel when she drifted off. We packed two flasks of Jelly Feel Real and a wooden crate of dragon fruit that Angel bought from a Poly kid in our building. When Angel tried to start up her little Saxo it didn't even cough. It didn't do anything, and Angel dragged her hands through her hair and said she didn't know why she was even surprised. It hadn't been driven in eighteen months. Then the engine started, just like that, as if it had been jerked from a deep sleep. Angel laughed and cracked open a Jelly Feel Real for the journey.

Angel sees Casper every week as well. He was the one who suggested we live together. Casper studied Psychiatry at a school in Melbourne, which is the seventeenth best school in the world. At first it made me feel a bit like I was eating chocolate éclairs with a celebrity, until I realised that he is clumsy and laughs at all kinds of childish things. Now it just feels like eating chocolate éclairs with someone who isn't Angel. We used to talk about my big brother Sunny, and the boat trip, and my time at Christmas Wood Refugee Detention Centre, but now he just asks how much I'm getting out of the house, and I try not to exaggerate too much, and then we talk about how Angel is getting on and all the bull-dust that's been on the teev lately. I told Casper I can't imagine why he would have wanted to leave a place like Melbourne to live on a tiny island that is famous for nothing except for being covered in dead crabs. He said that he needed to be around people who are motivated. No creature is more motivated than a Red Island crab who wants to migrate for breeding. Even if they do all get run over.

I told him that it was no wonder there were so many mad people on an island where the dominant species suffers a mass genocide each year in its quest for sex, and he laughed so hard he spilt his coffee.

When we drove to the island ferry port, I would never have guessed that Angel hadn't been behind a wheel in so long. She drove with her seat pushed way back and her knees at the wheel, so she could do her daily Sudoku in the paper when we got stuck in traffic. Her ribs worked alarmingly beneath her tie-dyed t-shirt. That's all Angel ever wears; tie-dyed t-shirts that she violently stretches to turn them into little dresses. We wound all the windows down because it was hot as well as stormy. She grinned at me and flicked on the radio, switching it quickly whenever reports came on about the war. She told me to *Smile, baby, because we were leaving the island and I was going to see a Red Island crab the right way up for once.*

Angel is my best friend on Christmas Island. She used to be called Taliska Nguyen. When she was twenty she was sent home from work sick, where she lay in bed and watched an English video she had picked up from a thrift store; a cartoon called Angelmouse. She decided that Angelmouse was the most fundamentally virtuous being ever created, and she quit her job as the box-kid for a dessert company, and changed her name to Angel Mouse in search of being a better person. The Australian government decided that when a depressive, cataplectic twenty-year-old Polynesian girl quits her job and legally changes her name to Angel Mouse, it's not an epiphany, it's a disability. She was put on the same disability benefits scheme as me.

When we got on board the ferry, Angel dragged me to the back of the boat to lean over the painted white railings and watch the foam at the back of the boat. Christmas Island was quick to disappear. I didn't think much of the Euphrates, except that it occurred to me that I'd only ever seen three large bodies of water. The Euphrates river, this stretch of ocean that I had crossed when I was ten, and again now, and the stinking billabong by Passion Flower, covered in garbage and blowies. Angel grabbed my hand and we went to the boat-bar and asked for Jelly Feel Reals, sunny-side up; red on top, cream underneath. Just like a Red Island crab, still alive.

Angel loves Jelly Feel Real cocktails. She heats rice pudding every morning for breakfast, and the sugary smell of it covers up the stink of dirty laundry and poppers that usually fills our building. Then she has a dragon fruit at midday, and about a hundred Jelly Feel Reals between then and night-time. I met her two years ago when Casper gave me a confidence exercise, and I had to go and introduce myself to someone in the waiting room. She was sprawled out across three chairs, digging chunks of white flesh out of half a dragon fruit with her penknife. The first thing that I noticed was how skinny she was. Not pretty skinny, like the girls in magazines, just sort of hollow, with grey cheek-bones and a fine layer of fur over her limbs. Not that I'm in a position to judge. I'm so small that when I sit in Casper's chair my feet don't even reach the floor. Casper says he thinks I chose to talk to Angel because she looks like me, as though she could be Iraqi or from somewhere close. Angel says she thinks I chose to talk to her because good souls seek each other out. I think it's just because she was closest to the door of Casper's office.

We arrived in Perth on time but the journey to the aquarium took a while. I sort of forgot why we were going. I forgot to be excited about finally seeing Red Island crabs that were alive. I sat in front of a jerky stand with my head on my knees for around an hour, while Angel stayed huddled at her wheel in the parking lot with the engine running, trying to stay warm. I cried for a long time, mainly because of Sunny, and Angel fell asleep with her head on the passenger seat. Eventually I looked up to see her leave the car and go into a bar on the sea-front called The Liquid Zoo. By the time she came back I had got back into the car. She smelt strongly of raspberry cordial and Malibu, and she had another roll of ten dollar bills, but wouldn't say where they'd come from. As we drove to the aquarium, she started crying. I've never seen Angel cry. It's not because she's strong, it's because she just doesn't know how. The sunlight between the city buildings lit up the tears that quivered along her jaw. I told her I didn't know if she was crying because of the war in Iraq, or because I made her cold, and she said she wasn't crying because of the war, or the cold, she was crying because it must be so horribly painful to be me. Then we got lost for a long time.

Angel and I live in Passion Flower Affordable-Housing Complex, P.F. for short, but someone has sprayed the front of the building to change it to Perverts and Fobs, which is kind of true, because the first three floors of the building are owned by the jail and are used as a half-way house, and most of the people who live here are Polynesian. Beneath that it says b4i√uru>16, which I might find kind of witty if I was anyone who isn't me. We are both in what the council calls

Unreliable Slash Irregular Employment. That means they will keep paying our disability benefits as long as we don't receive wages. Angel makes tables out of used electric guitars, and young bohemian couples buy them for their new apartments. She only makes one every few months but people pay crazy dollar for them. Usually $500, for an inconveniently-shaped table made out of rubbish. And we're supposed to be the mentally ill ones. People always ask why we don't have a guitar table in our own living room, and Angel tells them that she can't afford not to sell them all. But really it's because she hates them, just as she hates anything that isn't what she describes as utilitarian.

I sort of work for Amnesty International. They pay me to write to other young refugees and be a sympathetic ear when they struggle to fit into Australian culture. It's a bit of a joke really. I don't even speak Kurdish any more.

When we finally reached the front of the queue at the aquarium, we asked the lady at the desk where the Red Island crabs were. She looked confused and asked if we meant the giant Spider crabs. We were directed past a sign that read Get Lost in Amazonia, which seemed pretty rude to me, and we had to walk through plastic leaves and vines, past dark tanks whose plaques boasted of rare eels, but appeared empty. By the time we reached the Red Island Crabs my hands were wet where they gripped onto Angel's fingers. They weren't even in a proper tank. They just lived in two glass pillars half-filled with water that were either side of a little bridge. They were just decorations. And they were purple. There was a little sign next to one of the pillars which explained that the purple ones were a much rarer type of the same species. I pressed my face up against the glass and watched the groups of them pile on top of each other on harshly-lit rocks. They slumped over their crooked legs like quivering old men. The ones that had risen in the water were awkwardly buoyant, hobbling on their missing claws.

The night we moved into our apartment in Passion Flower, Angel and I lay down on a bare mattress in the bare living room, and Angel stuck a candle in an empty wine bottle and asked me why I didn't die when the refugee boat crashed into Flying Fish Cove. I told her it was because I had been thrown overboard along with a bunch of other kids twenty minutes before, in protest to the Australian government for not letting the boat dock. She said that my parents must have been selfish fuckers to try and sacrifice me like that. She was the first person not to look awkward and pat my hand in confused sympathy. I love that girl.

At the crab tank Angel told me to *Smile, Casper wanted evidence*, and she snapped me with a disposable camera. Then she asked me why I was crying again. I turned my face away from her to face a tank of crudely gold and silver fish. I looked at the plaque which said they were angelfish and pointed them out to Angel, and she wrinkled her nose at them. She said they looked like they'd been wrapped in tin foil, and she preferred the ones opposite. She pressed her nose to a big round tank of glass catfish. They were nothing more than skeletons with eyes, their flesh entirely transparent. They were empty, all the way to the core, poised in the current in a small cluster; resolute. I was feeling pretty mad about the crabs being purple, and I tried to get Angel to come with me to the touch tank, but she stayed with her nose pressed to the glass catfish and shook me off. I stalked off between the plastic vines, getting confused by cunningly placed mirrors, until the darkness became too much and I lay down on one of the little bridges next to a fake billabong. There was a huge archway of water above me full of pale pink and orange orbs, like pulsing flames. Moon jellyfish. They hung in the water, tiny, violent and iridescent.

I think Angel could have been rich if she wanted. A year ago she spent a while experimenting with different things to add to rice pudding, fats and preservatives and so on, until she had perfected durable emergency food in a package. She moulded it into little lumps and wrapped it in tin foil. She called it Angel Mouse Cake, and the Australian Red Cross changed its name to Plumpi-Nut and gave her $20,000 for it. We spent two days in our room with glossy catalogues, deciding where to move to with the money, then on the third day Angel gave me some Valium and sent me to the milk bar for raspberry cordial, and by the time I came back she had posted a cheque to the ARC for $20,000, and we stayed right where we were, which I was pretty relieved about because moving sounds like a pretty huge nightmare to me.

On the drive home I tried to fall sleep with my head against the window. Angel shoved me so that my head bumped the glass and said *Don't sleep doll, what if I pass out? All our little babies will die,* and she giggled, and flashed a mermaid's purse in front of my face, bulging with fish eggs. Angel never could go anywhere without stealing something from someone. I once asked her if she thought Angelmouse would ever steal, and she shrugged and said *I bet Angelmouse wouldn't judge a poor, sad Poly girl for taking a souvenir or two to remind her of the good times, seldom as they are.* Just the smell of the salt water was enough to make me want to stay away from the Island forever.

I hang onto pieces of Sunny like you wouldn't believe. He is serious in every memory, the permanent crease of a frown over his left brow. *Nobody can bring you peace, Fallon,* he told me. He was saying things like that long before the war.

The day after we got back from Perth I showed Casper the picture Angel took of me standing next to the tube of purple crabs, looking small and tearful and serious behind my round-spectacles, and he laughed and clapped his hands together. I think he would have hugged me but I don't touch anyone except Angel. I didn't tell Casper about Angel crying, or about her getting too cold in front of the jerky stand. Angel isn't allowed to get cold. She can't warm up for days and it makes her go a bit funny, she just hugs her belly and won't talk to anyone. Then Casper got me to do a progress exercise, and write down three things that were keeping me happy.

1.) There is nothing left of mine that the war can destroy.
2.) There are Red Island Crabs that are alive, even if they are purple, and there are also moon jellyfish which are about a thousand times prettier.
3.) I made it to Perth and back again.

On the way back from Casper's office I went to the milk bar to get more dragon fruit for Angel. The horizon rumbled in a way that, before the trip to Perth, would have scared me. But you have to be sensible about things like storms, and crabs, and all your dead relatives. I stopped on the front step of the bar, instead of darting inside like usual. I looked up somewhere just past the sky, and didn't kid myself for a moment that Sunny was anywhere close by, and yet Angel was always somewhere next to me, with a sly grin and her pockets full of mermaid's purses. The storm hung above, me, waiting, like a great moon jellyfish.

Melanie Whipman

Melanie lives in a leafy Surrey village with her husband, teenage twins, dog, cats and chickens. Much to her amazement, this is her second story to be featured in a Bristol Short Story Prize Anthology. She has an MA in Creative Writing and is currently a PhD student at the University of Chichester. When Melanie's not researching or attempting to write she teaches Creative Writing for the ACL. Her short stories have been published online and in magazines and anthologies and her first novel was longlisted for the Cinnamon Press Award. Sadly, it now inhabits slush piles across the country, so she's recently turned her attention to a second novel.

After the Flood

I can't sit still these days. Noah shakes his head and says an arse the size of mine is designed for sitting on. But I can't – settle.

'I miss the ark.' I say, and he gives me that look and raps his knuckles on the side of my head, like he's trying to knock out the memories.

Noah used to miss it too. For months he walked around like a land-locked fisherman, eyes searching the horizon, legs too wide, feet ready for a tipping board. Now he strides, with the long, earth-eating gait of someone who knows he's saved the world.

Last week some bloke calls round, asking for an interview. My home-help delivers the message. She stands at the bedroom door, raises her voice so he cannot fail to hear her from the hallway, 'There's some word-monger asking for you. He's persistent.'

'Are you having a laugh?' I say, 'Aren't they all fed up with it by now? A story this old?' But I heard his voice, through the window, low and throaty, so I tell Sheila to send him down to the vineyard to find Noah. 'After lunch,' I say, 'Then he'll talk.' He likes to taste his wine with the meal. He's easy then, mellow with grape juice and a full stomach.

'No,' she says, hands on her hips, mouth curved in a disgruntled rainbow, 'It's your story he wants.'

'My story?' I fiddle with the shell in my lap, hold it against my ear for a second.

'What shall I tell him then?'

I lay the conch back on the bedside table. 'That I don't do interviews, don't have a story. Nothing happened. Noah listened to God, I listened to Noah. My husband built it, loaded it, sent out the doves. I just fed the animals. Tell him to find Noah, he's the one who likes talking. And tell him to ask about the vineyard. There's a story. He created it, first vineyard in the world. He can see him there, taste his wine...'

Sheila's hands slip from her hips to her apron pocket, she stares at me. Her twisting fingers look like something trapped.

'What was it like? You never say.'

If I close my eyes I can still hear it. The creaking of the timber, the slap of the water, the grunts and squeaks and whinnies and squawks. It's the silence here I find – difficult. The stillness. I have a shell in every room now, collected them one by one over the years. When I walk through the house I hold them to my ear, listen to the sea trapped inside.

'Mrs Noah?'

'I don't remember.'

I can't sit still these days, I pace and pad about this space and dream of things I shouldn't. Noah scowls and shakes his head and tells me in his soap-box-voice to quit my fidgeting. He gives me his spiel about not confusing motion with action. But there's no action for me to take, the children are long gone, there's Sheila to do the housework, and Noah tends the fertile soil of his vineyard and drinks his wine. That's what I loved about the Ark – the constant motion but no action, no decisions. We'd done all that, fifty-two years of Noah listening, and planning and chopping the cedars and building and cooking and smoking and packing the food and getting all the animals in. Then there was just the water and the waiting. A state of limbo, but for once something you didn't have to feel guilty about.

This last month Noah's changed. There's something missing. He watches my pacing in silence, his eyes clouded and cunning. I wait for his moods, those violent flashes, like a thunderstorm at sea, all threat and menace before he lashes out. But now he sits and stares at me, brooding, swollen with malice and wine. When we have sex he takes me from behind, wordless until it's over. 'Don't pretend you don't like it,' he says afterwards.

I should never have told him.

'Mrs Noah?'

He's at the gate, leaning over, eyebrows raised. I recognise the gravelly voice, the man from last week. He's disappointing in the flesh, a porridge face, too-quick to smile, one hand on the latch, the other held forward in greeting. If he had a hat he'd take it off. I look around for Sheila but it's market day.

'My husband's at the vineyard.' I don't think he is. Lately he's taken to eating meat again. He polishes his spears, goes out hunting, brings me home the bodies, feathered and furry. Dumps them on the draining board, 'Don't pretend you don't like it,' he says. This morning he was up with the first thread of birdsong. I watched him from the window, striding across to the barn in the milky dawn. His body stiff and purposeful. All action.

'I'm meeting your husband later. It's you I wanted to see. Just a few words, about your experience on the ark – as a wife.' He's walking up the path now, his eyes flicking past the courgettes and beans and alfalfa, 'They say you're a vegetarian?' He stands in front of me, hand shoved out, takes mine in a double-palmed clasp, like I'm some old friend. Fake idiot, but I like the way his eyes don't shift from my face when he sees the bruises.

'Just a couple of minutes,' he says.

'The water's on the boil, you can have some tea.'

'So what was it like?'

'What bit?' I look him straight in the eye, wait for him to ask how I felt leaving my family and friends behind, whether I begged Noah to save them when the rain began to fall, what I did when he stood there on the shifting deck, listening to some invisible voice, bloated with I-told-you-sos.

He runs his fingers along the grain of the table, 'Were you scared? Noah said there were storms, violent storms.'

'He hated the storms.'

'Did the animals panic?'

It was Noah who panicked. I was always ready for it, you knew when it was coming, there was that change in the air first. You'd take a breath and there'd be the sharp taste of salt, like blood, on your tongue, and a billowing blackness on the horizon, blocking out the world. You'd feel the weight of it, and the boards beginning to tip, and Noah would be all ranting fury and prayers spat out like blasphemy. 'What the fuck d'you want now? Haven't I done enough?' I'd leave him to it, head down to the Ark's dark belly, with the animals. He'd be there waiting for me and I'd bury my face in the salty softness of his mane, hold him close until the thunder and the shrieking wind and Noah's moans were drowned out by his great rattling purr.

'Were you scared?'

'No.'

'What about the animals? What was it like living with them? They say Noah was attacked by a lion once...'

I should never have told Noah about him. I've lost my wifely arts, my feminine guile, once upon a time I'd have sealed my secret, but these days I can't keep him off my mind, off my tongue. I told him a month ago. 'Noah,' I said, not taunting or attention-seeking, but with the right degree of humbleness, real, not feigned. 'Noah, forgive me, I've sinned.'

It felt like no sin. That honeyed hide beneath my thighs and the dandelion down of his stomach. Nothing was ever so soft. You could blow it away with one whispered kiss. And the bat of his paw. Like the brush of butterfly's wings. And when I think of Noah's cuffs... Not that I have any right to complain now. What did I expect?

'On the ark, did the lion attack?'

'He still has the scar. He'll show you if you ask.'

It was my fault, I didn't shut the gate properly, he came up when Noah was sick with rage. It's difficult being the only man on earth, when your God is silent and every whining, shifting wind brings the keening of the dead. He leapt on top of Noah, in one great golden bound, knocked him off me. They say he has a pride now, generations of them. I imagine lazy, loose-limbed lionesses and tubby cubs stretching in the desert sun.

'I will.' He dunks his biscuit, 'I'm seeing him later,' he holds it in too long and it drops with a spongey plop into the tea.

'He knows you've come here?'

'He suggested it. He was off hunting with some friends.'

He doesn't have real friends, they hang around him, watching and waiting, seeking signs in his drunken ramblings. How do they know he won't do it all over again? Won't leave them all to drown?

The man spoons up the sludgy mess in the bottom of his cup, peers at it and pops it into his mouth. He swallows and smiles, 'Noah was heading into the desert. There's been some old lion sniffing round. Stalking the women, one by one. Just waiting and watching. Reckons it'll attack soon.'

'So I heard.'

This morning Noah came into the bedroom, told me he was bringing me back a gift. 'Something special. You're going to love it,' he said, rattling the spears in his shoulder-pack and tugging at his beard all purpled with stale wine. I realised what was missing then – the listening. That look of perpetual distraction was gone.

'They're going to kill it,' the man gestures at the bare floor, 'It would look fine just here. Noah said he's bringing you back the pelt. A gift. I'm going to take a photo, write it up. D'you reckon it could be the same one? The one from the ark?'

I shrug and dunk my biscuit into my tea, pull it out before it falls. He found me last night, in the early hours, before Noah and the birds woke. He came through the open window in one great leap, the moon gilding his hide. I wrapped myself around him, inhaled the hot, stinking blast of his breath, let him rest his paw on my heart, lick me head-to-toe with his coarse-moist tongue and lap away my tears.

I could have gone with him, left Noah, but I've left enough people to drown.

I pick up the shell, hold it to my ear.

'Can you hear the sea?'

I shake my head and press the shell closer, listening to the far off roar of my lion.

Hilary Wilce

Hilary Wilce's stories have been published both here and in the United States, and have won the Ian St James Award, the Mathew Prichard Award and the Kent Literary Festival Award, as well as being shortlisted in the Bridport, Asham, Mslexia and Fish short story awards. She has just finished a young adult novel. She completed an MA in Creative Writing at Birkbeck three years ago, and since then her writing group of fellow students has been an invaluable support. By day she is a newspaper journalist specialising in writing about education, and also a personal development coach.

I Once Knew Salman Rushdie

I once knew Salman Rushdie. No, listen. I did. Long ago, before he was famous. And in all the years since, whenever I've seen him in the newspapers – his eyes hooded, his arm freighted with his latest woman – I always think of biscuit tins.

In fact, at a push, you could say he's the reason I'm standing here, on the edge of this damp November hockey pitch – even though all my adult life the bleakness of school playing fields has made me want to turn and bolt for home – thinking about the currents of our lives, and how little we control the things that snag at us as we pass by.

Out on the playing field my daughter is playing right wing. Her knees flash, her stick rummages, her ponytail flicks and bounces. I'm so proud of her, the way she goes back and back at the ball like a terrier at a rat. I could never have played the way she does. I played as if the only thing that mattered was how soon we could get back to the pavilion and into warm clothes.

I walk up and down with my shoulders hunched against the cold.

Good *pass*, St Dunstan's!

Take it *out!* Take it up the *wing!*

I've learned the language. Sometimes, quite carried away, I'll even shout: Go *Lucy!* And she will look over to me with a scowl that would shatter cannon balls and turn milk to cheese.

But Salman.

Salman and his biscuit tin.

It happened like this. Years and years ago, Salman was a university friend of my boyfriend, Mark, and later, after life had moved on and Mark and I had got together, another college friend of theirs would sometimes ask us all down to her parents' grand and fading Wiltshire home where we would sit and crunch small birds around the mahogany dining table, and Salman would hold forth on the evils of colonialism, staring from one to another of us with his hawk-like gaze, and no-one would ever dare interrupt him because what could we know, we gilded English boys and girls, of the oppressor's boot on a subjugated neck?

But Salman was boring. And I was far younger than everybody else around the table. So I would escape whenever I could to the kitchen, to wash and wipe, as did Salman's then wife and the mother of his baby, where together we'd have altogether a jollier time talking about anything that came to mind, and turning to tickle the baby's tummy as it sat round-eyed – it did not have its father's eyes – in its bouncer on the table.

Then one day I left something behind in Wiltshire, I can't remember what and the Rushdies brought it back for me, and I went to pick it up from them, from one of those quiet north London roads of Edwardian terraces, and had coffee in their kitchen and was offered a biscuit from their family biscuit tin full of jam circles and wafers and chocolate digestives, and as my hand reached out towards it, the thought flashed clear and bright through my brain that I, too, wanted a biscuit tin like that.

Our flat did not have such a tin. It did not have biscuits. It had fine olive oil and good coffee and headache pills for hangovers and not much else.

I was a journalist back then, getting about, and quite a long time after the biscuit tin moment I went to interview a rising young musician in Cambridge, and since she was at home on maternity leave we sat in her kitchen, among the muddle of her older children eating fish fingers and oven chips, and the pram, and the piles of picture books and the baskets of washing and I looked across at her fridge, studded with bright alphabet letters, and thought, just as suddenly: I want those too.

And so it was that the biscuit tin led to the alphabet numbers and in due course to our selling the olive oil flat and buying a house in Teddington, and getting married and producing our four rackety children, the last of whom is, on this drizzly November hockey pitch, now charging so fast towards the goal that I quite forget myself and shriek at the top of my voice: "Shoot, Lucy! *Shoot!*"

Eliciting a frown from a father standing just down the touch line from me, who has not, up to this moment, uttered even a cautious cheer.

Sometimes I wonder if Salman Rushdie ever remembers he had that biscuit tin.

Or that house in London. Or that wife. Although I'm sure he remembers those discourses on colonialism – the ones that made me so certain, all those years ago, that the kitchen was always as good a place, if not better, than the dining room.

But then what catches at my heart will never catch at his. Or yours. Or anyone else's.

I saw an old friend recently, one I hadn't seen for twenty years, who said: "You know, telling us about Wales was the best thing anyone ever said to us. We bought a house near St David's, and to the children it's been as much a home as Clapham."

And dimly I remembered how they had been fruitlessly hunting for a cottage in Dorset when I, fresh from a job on the Gower Peninsula, had cried with that moment's enthusiasm, 'Look in Wales! There's tons of places there.' And on that one careless cry their whole lives had turned.

What biscuit tins lurk in other people's minds? What cottages? What damp November playing fields?

Teddington.

Now there's a Place.

I should, of course, when I think of it, think of our family house, with its lemon hall and purple lilac tree and dog pee stain on the carpet in the family room that never came out no matter how hard I scrubbed at it.

But I think instead of genius. How it touches you on the wing, and you don't know it until later, if ever, because it takes genius to see genius before the world has officially declared it so, and this genius was a dull-looking man called Dr Vince Hall, in a green pullover, who worked in a government technical laboratory in Teddington among wires and boxes and circuit boards, and who I went to see for work, long, long before we ever moved there, and who took me first to see his computer – a huge whirring beast that needed a room of its own with a reinforced floor – and who then sat me down with a mug of weak tea and told me with fire in his eyes that soon – very soon – computers would be as small as a kitchen chopping board, if not smaller, and would handle photos and films and music as well as words and numbers, and link us all together in one giant, buzzing hive of information.

"What?" I said. "Even in my lifetime?"

"In your lifetime," he said – and I remember it so clearly, he spoke with the fervour of a Baptist preacher – "you will see things you cannot even now think possible. In your children's lifetime there will be things we cannot even yet conceive of."

To which I said, oh dull, dull me: "I don't have any children. Yet."

I wrote it down, and wrote it up, and thought no more about it, except that a few years later Dr Hall died tragically young of cancer, and was lauded in his obituaries as a man way ahead of his time, and now whenever I log onto the Internet or pick up my iPhone, I remember his green sweater and the fire in his eyes, and his weak government issue tea. And, of course, I remember Teddington, and the way that I had dimly registered, on my bus ride out to see him, that some of the streets there looked quite nice and that if in some unimaginable future one was ever to have a family, it was probably as good a place to bring up children as any.

Lucy doesn't score in her run towards the goal. The ball strikes the post and bounces out. The father on the touchline looks at me and I say, "I'm sorry. I get carried away sometimes. My daughter hates it when I shout." And there is a fleeting wry smile in his grey eyes that suddenly, out of nowhere, reaches down inside me and brushes my frozen heart.

I stand staring, touching my jacket, not sure what has just happened.

Then it is half time and the girls suck oranges with icy fingers, and it is my duty to swap sides and go round to the far side of the pitch where there is shrubbery and shadow, and then I do want to go home, I really do want to go home, but I can't. There is no choice. I have to stick it out and stay.

Lucy is our final child. Mark watched all the other children's matches. He watched in snow and hail and fog and rain. He loved it. He shouted like a maniac and never once, as far as I know, got a canonball stare. He didn't watch Lucy's matches because he was in a plane that crashed in Chennai in the monsoon rains when she was ten, and all that came home of his was a rusty and crumpled watch, so that then I had to do whatever I could to fill his absence in the family, although even to this day I can never bear to wear a watch, or even look at other people's.

Lucy says, about her matches: "Don't come. Nobody else's mother's does." But I tell her I have to, for her father's sake.

And for mine, too, although I never say it. And for my notion of what a family must be – bound close and warm together by biscuit tins and alphabet letters and carpet stains that won't come out.

That day, back on my own school hockey pitch, I remember it so well.

It was cold and raining. Our canvas boots squelched; our woollen socks scratched; our games mistress was her usual, sadistic self. It was a games lesson, not a match, and we were playing half-heartedly, and me even more so, because there was a lump in my stomach which wouldn't go away, in fact it got worse, so that in order to distract myself I looked hard first at this object, then at that. I remember seagulls tossing on a dirty winter sky, and the last few hazel leaves flapping, I thought, like prayer flags in the wind (we'd just seen a film on Tibet in geography). I remember someone's hollow footsteps, walking across the boards of the veranda of the pavilion, and the sound of a car crunching up the school gravel, far away across the tennis courts.

I remember being shouted at by the games mistress for missing an easy pass.

I remember thinking: this sickness, it's like dread. What am I dreading?

I remember the moment it got worse. The clammy hands. The sweating forehead. And running off into the shrubbery that edged the pitch.

Where I ran straight into a man behind a laurel bush, his flies wide open, his hand at his crutch.

And I remember that the shock of it stopped my sickness dead, so that I shouted out instead, and other girls came running, and I remember the man's look, blanched and scared, as he stared at their crowding, sniggering faces, and how he stumbled like an animal backwards, deeper into the bushes, with both hands clutching his trousers in place.

I don't remember much after that, although the story went immediately into our schoolgirls' book of myth and legend, and solemn warnings were issued from on high about girls being careful to avoid any dark and lonely places.

But what if the dark and lonely places are inside yourself?

What then?

I don't remember what it was that first made Mark want to go to India to make a film about the Chola bronzes. Something, one day, must have caught at his heart.

What I do remember is going home that afternoon after hockey with the sickness back in my stomach and finding our house even deader and colder than usual, and my mother alone in the kitchen, sitting in the winter dark, saying harshly, "You know it already, don't you? You know your father's gone and left us."

And later, bitterly, "Never rely on a man. Never. They'll always let you down in the end. Mark my words. They always will."

I didn't.

Mark never let me down. Never once.

He was let down by life.

And it has been so hard to lose him, hard beyond words. Beyond anything I can ever tell you.

These days we live in a smaller house, and not in Teddington, our lives squeezed for space if not for love, and when friends say, as they endlessly do: get out. You can't stay at home and mourn forever, I tell them I'm not. But that the only thing that matters to me now is that the children still live in a family that holds them safe and happy.

I swallow and watch the game flow past me until Lucy is a distant figure at the far end of the pitch. I pull my collar up against the cold, and feel the shrubbery at my back and let my eyes go to the father with the grey eyes walking up and down the touchline opposite.

I think about his smile, and how unexpectedly it arrowed into my heart.

I think of the sad and lonely man behind the laurel bush.

I think of Mark's watch, in its lidded box in the drawer in my bedroom.

I think of Salman Rushdie, and his many women, never slow to move from one to the next.

I think of Dr Hall and wonder what he would make of all that has flowed from his chopping board computers – the video clips and celebrity blogs and Facebook networks.

And I think of the dating website addresses that anxious friends have pressed on me, that I have always filed, so determinedly, in the bin.

And then, hugging my jacket, I look again at the man opposite me and suddenly think how perhaps I could, sometime when I'm ready, have a look at one or two. Just to see what they're all about, of course. Just for a laugh. Just because they're there.

Just because.

Samuel Wright

Samuel Wright is an English teacher. His son recently started crawling, which is bad news for his cat. His stories are frequently read at the Liar's League events in London, and have won prizes from Unbound Press, the Writers and Artists Yearbook, and *Spilling Ink*, as well as being published in *.Cent* and *Litro* magazines and coming third in the Bridport Flash Fiction Prize in 2011. He is currently collaborating on an art book about Hackney Marshes, and his writing can be found at http://bearsick.tumblr.com and @bearsick.

Symmetry

The dog was first. She ran into a metal post. For a split second he started to laugh, then his hand went to his mouth in shock.

He ran over. A Jack Russell had stopped for a piss near her head, but she was rigid. He knelt down and touched the side of her neck. A faint whine leaked out. Her black eyes were glassy, with white triangles at the edges. He slipped his hands underneath her body. The grass was cold and wet beneath them, but she was warm on his palms and the inside of his wrists. He lifted her. Her back leg hung fluidly.

At the vet's, he left her in the car. The waiting room was full of family units. Parent, child, pet. At first he sat. The chairs were small, like in a primary school. A girl with saliva on her lower lip and black shiny eyes like buttons looked up at him from the floor. He looked away, glancing uncomfortably up at the ceiling. When he looked back, she was still staring. She had a dog biscuit in her hand, and she raised it to her mouth without taking her eyes off him. He stood up and went up to the counter. He hovered for a moment behind a sick cat. He wanted to interrupt, say something to cut through all this crap, but he didn't know how to explain it.

"My dog… I've got her in the car. Should I… ?"

They went out to get her. They looked at her in the car, and she looked back out of the corners of her eyes. He pressed his hands tight under his arms. He could still feel her.

Once they had her inside, on the table, and they'd injected things in her, and she was still and breathing shallowly, they said they had to take the leg off. A very bad break, they explained, was hard to fix in dogs. But they would consult with another vet and give him all the options the next day.

He smiled and said thanks. He left her there and walked back out past the sick cats and the kids and the jangling bells and dog toys.

He got up early, five, and ran in the half-light. He ran for an hour, down streets and through the park. Trees arched in a tunnel around him. When he stopped he placed a hand under his thigh while he stretched and felt the heaviness of the muscle, the neatness and strength of it. He saw the skin ruckle over his knees, lined, but not sagging yet. He bent double and stared at his feet, brave in trainers, parallel.

When he went back, they said they could try to fix it. They could bolt and pin it, and she'd take a while to recover, and it was by no means certain, but they'd try it.

He looked at her. She was sedated, lying in a cage on her side. Asleep, you would have thought she'd be the same as ever, but she looked diminished and distant. He felt a stab of annoyance.

He said yes, try it.

So they cut open her leg, bolted it, pinned it. When she came back, it hung shaved and swollen. It seemed alien. She stood still, unsure what to do with it. Sometimes she sniffed it.

She had to stay in her cage. He spent long hours beside her, pottering, reading the paper, getting on with things, but increasingly just looking at her. She stared out blankly. Every now and then she would shift her weight from where she sat, and that stiff-necked, numb look would come across her and he'd find himself saying,

"Come on, girl, it's OK, come on now. You'll be OK soon. You've got to do this. It's for your own good."

Then he'd stop, and look at her. Her black brindle coat. Her paws, blunt. Her nose, rising to catch the invisible kaleidoscope of her world. And he'd speak again, in the same dutifully coaxing tone.

"Come on, you daft dog. You stupid dog. Do you think I've not got anything better to do."

Three weeks in, he was able to take her outside. They walked around the block, slowly. She held the leg up when she sped up, but if he kept it slow, her toes touched the ground, brushed it every step or two.

At first he stared at her the whole time. Then he looked up, as if he was just ambling, slowly, in the spring air. Blossom floated in dense branches above his head. The air was soft and dusty with a nip of cold swirled in amongst it. He shivered and crossed his arms while the dog gingerly pissed on a grimy tree root. His fingers rested on his thick arms, under the sleeves of his T-shirt. He felt goosebumps, and, on the right, a lump.

In the hospital, he sat bare-chested, while fingers probed. They put him in a tube, slid in and out like an airport X-ray. They found the bomb in his upper arm, a group of cells in open rebellion.

It was aggressive. They used the word, not him. Malignant, they said. Intent on causing harm. Sending out emissaries through his blood stream to spread revolt.

He thought of his arm, butchered, split into joints. He felt the ligaments that held him.

That night, he didn't keep the dog locked up. He led her carefully up the stairs to his bedroom, and into his bed. All night he felt her stiff shape next to him. He didn't sleep. When the light began to come through the curtains, he stared at his hand on the covers. The skin was grey, lined and shiny. Star-shaped creases spread across it, tessellating. He remembered when he had hated how young his hands looked, when they were smooth and fat and white.

Beyond where his hand lay, he saw the gleam of the dog's black eye, open, looking at him under a whiskered eyebrow.

They took the lump out. He had a sling. He showed the dog. She sniffed the stapled track curving across his arm.

On his walks, he held her leash in his left hand. Even when he no longer needed the sling, he rested his right hand in his jacket pocket. When she walked, she rested her foot fully on the ground.

He began to walk further. They ambled slowly together. He often felt unstable, like he might slip at any time, and fall, and if he fell, he might break. Standing under a tree, as the leaves spread in full summer green, he found his eyes wet. When people passed him, he looked away.

In the house, he took down his photos. He cleaned and reorganised, each time ending up with less and less stuff. In the evenings, he would cup the dog's haunches in his hands, and feel the asymmetry of her muscles. One leg was wasted and thin, the other tight with strength.

For six weeks, they blasted his arm with radiation until it blistered, then they told him they'd caught the cancer.

He called Alice to tell her, but hung up when she answered.

He began to keep a diary. Sometimes he wrote what he'd done that day, but soon it began to just be a record of his walks. Leaves he had seen, smells he thought the dog had caught.

One day, he realised he hadn't spoken to a human being for a week.

Now, his scar was fading. When the dog ran, it was almost as before. Out on the beach, she thundered across the packed wet sand in drumming arcs, then sprayed a turn through the dust of the dry dunes. She met the waves in rearing, turning caution, then fled as they broke on her.

His feet paced a heavy straight line while she danced around him.

On the cliff, where he always paused to watch the waves churn and slap, birds wheeled and perched. He watched a slick cormorant waddle on a rock, then dive up, catching the air and carving it in wingstrokes. When he was fifteen, he had shot a duck, and it had been the opposite – a swoop lurching down into a sudden lame flap on the mud.

As the walk ended, the dog lifted her leg more. The next day, her foot was swollen.

He began to dream about her. The dog in his dreams was half her, half not. Flickers of her mingled with himself, fur and eyes and strength flying airily through hazy fields. In the morning, when she greeted him with a wet face of flashed teeth and tongue, a soft nose and hair pressed tight, he felt in her eyes an echo of dreamed conversations, summit meetings between them where she told him reasoned secrets and he replied, barking.

Her foot stayed swollen.

When he saw her run, it was wrong. Her tail hung left, her feet thundered but with a slight skip. He ached to look at her.

The vet said the nerve was damaged. They gave him a dressing to put on her foot. She couldn't go in the water. They said again they might have to amputate.

Every night he bathed her foot in salt water. He held it gently, splayed the thick toes, worked the warm water into the round bore-holes of lesions that had punctured her rough pads. He threw away the first muddy water, then did it again, massaging her foot until his upper arm ached and he rubbed at that instead. Then he carefully dressed it in a cloth sock. She worried at it, and he smacked her when he caught her.

He locked her in again. He sat beside her and spoke through the bars. He tried not to listen to what he said. At night, on his own in bed again, his fingers traced the scar on his arm, touching, then drawing back, then touching again, each time checking but not checking.

When they walked, she strained. The high summer was turning into autumn, and she stretched her neck out to tempting clumps of leaves hiding secrets. He pulled in tight, checked her dressing, made her rest the alien foot on the ground.

He went to the beach, once. He intended to keep her on the leash, and just watch the waves. They stood at the top of the dunes. She half-sat, nose in the air. His left hand sat on her shoulder, and he caught a wisp of a dream conversation. He unhooked the leash, and watched her, his right hand in his pocket.

She ran down the dune in a cloud of sand. He watched her wheel and brake against the flat pane like a fly against a window. She hurled into the waves, raising spray around herself and letting the cresting sea break over her head-on.

When she ran back to him, the dressing was gone and her foot was bleeding. Her mouth cracked in a panting grin, and she stood foursquare and symmetrical as the blood leaked down unnoticed.

They took it off a week later. His dreams were fevered butcher's blocks. His joints felt loose. When he picked her up from the vet's her face cracked wide at him and her long nose nuzzled close. He didn't look properly until they were home. Then, he sat beside her as she stood and he stared at the missing part of her.

He closed his eyes and rose to his feet.

While he cooked his meal, she sniffed around him. He didn't look at her. He watched the knife in his hands cutting carrots, and stared at the soft, lined flesh of his right arm. He paused, holding the knife. He looked down at her, lop-sided, shaved and puckered up with staples. He remembered being fifteen, standing on the neck of the duck he had shot.

He lowered himself to the ground.

She stared at him. He raised both hands to her ears, and rubbed them. He rubbed in circles round the ears and neck, raising her hair in messy tufts. Her coat felt rough and greasy to his touch. He felt the cold tiles underneath him, and the warmth of her skin through the coarse fibres of her hair. Her breath stank out of her open mouth. Her eyes were black pebbles, staring vacantly while her nose hoovered up smells hungrily from his neck and face.

He reached out a hand to where her leg had been. It was gone from high up in her thigh. He cupped his hand around the space without touching her. She turned and stared at what he was doing. Her nose poked into his hand and her tongue slipped into his palm. He pulled away, and her tail wagged, and she stared short-sightedly into his face, inches away from him, and barked.

Her stumpy back end waggled so hard her one foot skittered on the tiles.

He slept alone that night. In the morning he called Alice.

Judges' profiles

Ali Reynolds (Chair)

Ali previously worked as an editor at Vintage, Random House, where she commissioned collections of short stories and novels from emerging writers. She moved to Bristol to establish her own literary consultancy in 2005. A passionate advocate for the creativity and talent in Bristol, Ali is involved with the Bristol Festival of Literature and runs masterclasses for creative writers. Ali has been involved with the Bristol Short Story Prize since 2010 and has been thrilled to see it evolve into the internationally recognised competition it is today. She lives with her husband and two children, who are bookworms like herself. www.alireynolds.co.uk.

Bidisha

Bidisha is a writer, critic, broadcaster and human rights activist who has been writing professionally since she was 14 and signed her first book deal at 16. She writes about the arts and social issues for *The Guardian, The Observer, The Financial Times, The F Word* and many other publications internationally. She has been the presenter of *Night Waves* (Radio 3), *The Strand* (World Service), *Woman's Hour* and *Saturday Review* (both Radio 4) and numerous arts documentaries for the BBC. She judged the Orange Prize in 2009 and the *John Llewellyn Rhys Prize* in 2010. Her reportage book *Beyond the Wall: Writing A Path Through Palestine* was published earlier in 2012.

Anna Britten

Anna Britten is an author and journalist. Her short stories have been broadcast by BBC Radio 4, published in the *Bridport Prize Anthology 2010*, the Bloomsbury anthology *Is This What you Want?* (via the Asham Award), *Decongested Tales*, and on US websites *Eclectica* and *Prick Of The Spindle* – and shortlisted for various other competitions including the Fish International. She has also published non-fiction and children's fiction. Twitter: @msabritten.

Christopher Wakling

Christopher Wakling's six acclaimed novels include *What I Did* (John Murray, 2011) and *The Devil's Mask* (Faber, 2011). He is the Royal Literary Fund Writing Fellow at Bristol University, leads Creative Writing courses for the Arvon Foundation, and writes travel journalism for *The Independent*. Before he turned to writing full time, Christopher worked as a city lawyer, and before that he read English at Oxford. He lives in Bristol with his wife and children.

Acknowledgements

A big thank you to the following people for their brilliant contributions to this year's Bristol Short Story Prize:

This year's judges – Ali Reynolds (chair), Anna Britten, Bidisha, Chris Wakling; our readers – Katherine Hanks, Helen Hart, Lu Hersey, Tania Hershman, Richard Jones, Marc Leverton, Mike Manson, Dawn Pomroy; Arts Council England; Chris Hill, Jonathan Ward, Sami Al-Adawy and the 3rd year Illustration students at University of the West of England; Meg White, Andy Gove, Anna Wredenfors, Simon Gould, John Bennett and pupils at Fairfield, Henbury and Redland Green schools, Jane Guy and The Bristol Hotel, Peter Begen and Arnolfini, Joe Burt, Funky Dog, Mark Furneval, Fran Ham, Mel Harris at Waterstones, Nicky Johns, Sylvie Kruiniger, Jonathan Lewis, Kathy McDermott, Natasha Melia, Sam Morrison, Peter Morgan, James Murray-White, Dave Oakley, and to all the writers whose short stories have given us so much pleasure and inspiration.